The *Runaway* Witch's Kiss

Spellbound Underground #1

Tamela Miles

ISBN: 978-1-68046-959-2

Published by Satin Romance
An Imprint of Melange Books, LLC
White Bear Lake, MN 55110
www.satinromance.com

Cover Design by Caroline Andrus

A sincere thank you to all of my writing partners who help me, even in the witching hour, shape my messes into masterpieces. You are deeply appreciated. This is also for every little, misunderstood black kitty who crosses my path—I have treats for you.

ONE

Nahla sat in the tub of warm water, focusing on the painted happy faces on both of her big toes poking out above the bubbles. They were a big lie. She wasn't happy at all, more like deeply dissatisfied at the direction her life had suddenly and drastically taken. She reached for the bottle of fragrant body wash, wincing at the pain in her arm. She rubbed the ugly bruises already forming, grimacing.

Tonight, Sebastian had finally done what she had feared he would do for months. He had dared to put his hands on her during an argument. It hadn't been about money, like normal couples, even though he was prone to lavish spending. She figured, since it was mostly his money to spend, to keep silent on the subject. The bills were always paid on time so she had little to be concerned about. No, this argument stemmed from the root of their problems—his possessive and jealous nature. Her simple decision to have a coffee and catch up with an old friend had set him off in a way she had never seen.

This has been building up for a long time, she reasoned with herself. Tonight's argument turning physical should have been no surprise, yet Sebastian's volatile response had still caught her off guard. She rubbed her face with the washcloth, wiping away tear stains. What could happen next? Would he actually strike her? A big part of her said to get out now before she found out the answer. *But, I love him…* Another part of her spoke the truth and it stung. She was also deeply invested in their relationship, having given up most aspects of her busy life to build a future with him. Her mind swirled in confusion. If only there was some way she could reassure him and finally put to bed all of his insecurities about her love and loyalty.

Her phone pinged on the bathroom countertop, but she made no move to check it. A moment later, she heard footsteps in her bedroom, right outside the bathroom. The door slowly creaked open and Sebastian came in. "Leave me alone." Her voice cracked with suppressed hurt and anger.

He tousled his blond hair with a quick hand and offered her one of his usual charming smiles. So, his mood had apparently improved and now he expected all to be forgiven. "I see you're still mad about me being a bit overprotective."

Her tone was tight. "No. I'm pissed because you escalated a simple argument. You grabbed my arms and slammed me back against a wall, Sebastian."

He waved a hand. "So, I overreacted. I promised you it'll never happen again. There's no room in our life together for other men. I told you that from the start. I—

I guess the idea of you spending time, even having a coffee, with someone else pushed all my buttons and I went crazy with jealousy."

She heaved a deep sigh. "But, there's no reason to be jealous."

He strode over to stand above her, stroking her forehead

with his fingers. "Look more closely in the mirror, Nahla. I have every reason to be jealous. You're beautiful. Other men want to own you."

She batted his fingers away impatiently and met his gaze squarely. 'If you lay a hand on me again, I'm gone. No explanations, no excuses—I'll be in the wind." Her phone pinged again.

"I take it we're both settling in for the evening."

She shook her head. "No, I'm going to see my Mom."

His lips flattened and his gaze went cold. He put his back to her and swiped her phone from the counter. "Not tonight. You're staying right here. I won't hurt you again, but I mean what I say. I always come first in this relationship. Your mother can see you some other day."

Nahla swiftly rose up, stepping out of the tub. She scrambled to catch his arm as he headed out. "No!" The door closed firmly in her face and she heard the grating of the lock from the outside. She tried the handle. Son of a bitch, he had locked her in again.

In her bedroom, she heard him chuckle loudly as he headed down the hallway. She pounded on the door and shouted for long moments. Wrapping her arms around her body, she struggled to stand as the trembling began all through her. He could come back in a few minutes or as long as an hour and, all the while, she had to fight the forceful panic of being trapped. Sinking to the floor, she let the tears drip down her face.

TWO

Three Months Later

"THIS IS SOMETHING A PAID WHORE WOULD WEAR," NAHLA muttered in disgust, gripping the item in question. She tossed the black leather bodysuit, crotchless with nipple cut-outs, back on the luxurious bed and snorted. Her new husband of a few months had a rude surprise coming, if he thought otherwise. Nahla had no intention of changing out of her comfy, plush navy robe. She re-read his note, her annoyance rising, before crumpling it up in a ball and throwing it on the carpeted floor.

She looked around the elegant bedroom they shared, tastefully decorated in earth tones. She and Sebastian had worked hard over the past few months to make their classic townhome, in Pasadena, a place of relaxation and stylish comfort as they began their new lives together. Her hand rubbed across her small baby bump and she focused on the clock on the polished wood nightstand. He was coming home later and later, she noted. His schedule was always full of new clients and business meetings, but she tried to be understanding, brushing off her doubts. His salacious gift of the bodysuit to her tonight only raised her suspicions.

Nahla rested on the end of the bed, rubbing her tired feet. She regretted not attending her friend, Jeff's birthday bash this evening, but Sebastian insisted she stay home to spend time with him. She and Jeff both worked as administrative assistants in the same high-rise office building in Downtown Los Angeles. She had been working steadily, as well as finishing her masters degree in marriage and family counseling, long before she met her husband.

Sebastian had come into her life almost a year ago, whirling her off her feet with promises of love and a good life if she would just give in to him. When Nahla learned she was pregnant with his child, they hastily married at his insistence of providing a perfect and stable life for her and the baby. Many warlocks, like him, were traditional and 'did the right thing'. *But, have I done the right thing by marrying him,* she mused.

They came from two different witch covens, different worlds. Nahla grew up as a young witch in a more middle-class home and neighborhood, with a focus on family values. Sebastian's world was flashier, with money to throw around. It hadn't mattered to her, in the beginning of their relationship, but she was now feeling the strain on their new marriage.

Nahla was instantly alert when she heard the door open downstairs. Her anger rising, she snatched up the bodysuit, padded down the hallway, and stood at the top of the stairs. Sebastian locked the door and looked up. She noted that he had ditched his tie and his collar was askew. His short blond hair was disheveled. She narrowed her eyes and threw the bodysuit on the steps. She headed back to the bedroom, with him on her heels.

When he followed her, she whipped around. He reeked of woman's perfume, not her own. He held the bodysuit up and approached her. She backed up, reeling from the pain of his probable infidelity. "I'm less than pleased with your little gift. Why don't you give it to the whore you were with tonight?" Her tone was pure acid.

Sebastian's lips lifted in an amused grin. "Your jealousy is touching but unfounded. I told you this would be a late night. I had a business meeting." He raised the bodysuit. "I expected you to greet me wearing this."

Nahla's glare could cut glass. "Not in this lifetime, Sebastian. You're covered in perfume and you look like you just rolled out of someone's bed." She moved around him, heading to the bathroom. She would not cry in front of him, she swore to herself. "If I had known this earlier, I could've spent the night at Jeff's party, talking to him."

In the next moment, Sebastian gripped her arms roughly. He whirled her around and shoved her down onto the bed. As she stared at him in shock, he pinned her down with one hand and gripped her face with the other. The chill in his eyes stroked her spine.

"Since we're married, you're essentially my property, Nahla. You and that baby belong to me. If I say you're no longer able to talk to your little friend, Jeff, then believe I mean it. I'm disappointed you don't like my gift. Maybe I will give it to another woman, one who's appreciative and willing, like you used to be."

Tears rolled down Nahla's cheeks, but her expression was defiant as she met his eyes. Her voice was hoarse. "You don't own me, and you don't own my baby. God, I wish I never married you. Living with you is hell. It's either your way or the highway, right?"

He released her and shrugged. "You may as well get used to the way things are. It's only my way. The highway isn't an option for you, especially since you're having my child." He headed for the door, speaking over his shoulder. "I'm going back out. Try to be in a better mood when I get back."

Nahla heard him go down the staircase and out the front door before she raised up on the bed. She dashed away tears with the back of her hand, resolve setting in. The reality of her nightmare marriage only ignited her to change things. Damn it, she would not be treated like his property and she definitely did not want this horrible life for her child. It was time to do something about the situation.

She unplugged her cell phone from the charger and tapped the screen. In a few moments, her mother's voice was in her ear. "Mom, I need your help…"

———

"Oh, my beautiful girl." Gilda Gregory shook her head, wearing a pained expression on her smooth brown face. "I did try to warn you away from Sebastian Caldecott because I sensed nothing good from him. His aura is black as tar."

Nahla grasped her mother's hand tightly. She had hurriedly dressed in a colorful sundress and packed a large tote bag of whatever clothing and toiletries she could grab after Sebastian left. Upon loading up her white Jeep, a gift from him, she realized that as much as she loved it, she would have to leave it behind. "I see that now, Mom. I just wish…" her voice trailed off.

"That he would change?" Gilda snorted. "There's no spell to cure being a bastard."

Nahla shook her head. "No. I know he will never change so there's no point looking to magick for a miracle."

Her mother went on. "Anytime a man is always gone on business trips and barely leaves time for his wife, especially a pregnant one, he's cheating. And, he put his hands on you."

Nahla nodded. "That was the end for me. I knew that I couldn't live in that toxic environment with him. He's always been controlling so I should've seen this coming. No way am I bringing my child into all that."

Gilda's smile was comforting. She ruffled her daughter's lush, long brown curls, identical to her own. "I raised a ninja, not a docile princess-type."

She gave a small laugh, absently rubbing the sore bruise near her lips. "So, I've done some thinking. Your house is the first place he'll come looking for me. I need to disappear. Literally. I have to get off his radar completely. His magick is strong enough to track me if I don't do some sort of cloaking spell."

"Which we'll do together." Her mother's tone was adamant. "We're about to have some serious magick going on in here. Did you remember to bring your grandma's spell book?"

"It's in my bag." She rose from her chair at the table in the brightly decorated kitchen. "I'll go get it." In a moment, she was back, setting down the huge, archaic tome of spells with a thud. She caressed the old leather.

"Before we get to spell casting, I have an ideal solution to this problem that may work." Gilda leaned in close. "Your dad and I, before he passed on, used to be a part of a large, hidden network that offered assistance to witches in dire circumstances. It's still operating today. It's called Spellbound Underground."

Nahla frowned. "Why am I just now finding out about this…underground?"

Gilda waved a hand. "Not meant for kids to know about. Besides, you never needed to know about it before today."

"What kind of help can they give me?"

Gilda's laughter tinkled. "You, my sweetheart, will completely disappear. The underground coven will make sure of that. It could take several months for Sebastian to find you and, by then, the baby will be born. You'll have strong ground to stand on regarding custody and a divorce from him."

Nahla made up her mind in five seconds flat. "I want Spellbound Underground to help me, even though this feels like witness protection."

"Wonderful! After we do the spell casting from your grandma's book, I'll make the calls to my contacts." Gilda rose from her chair and beckoned to her daughter. "Let's get the things we need from my special closet and get started."

Nahla laughed. "Your "Closet of Shadows"?"

Gilda's smile warmed her heart and calmed her anxiety.

Later, they sat on a black mat marked with white chalk to form a witches' circle in the middle of the living room. Gilda had closed the drapes as Nahla lit the candles and incense sticks. The setting was conducive to a peaceful frame of mind. She gently opened her grandmother's spell book, immediately turning to one of the many bookmarked pages.

Nahla began chanting in a murmur, welcoming the spirits hanging about in an ancient language. Her mother grasped her hand and chimed in. Moments later, a small wind kicked up in the room and the candles flickered wildly. "Alright, Mom. Let's do some serious magick."

Gilda gripped Nahla's hands in her own as a small whirlwind fluttered the book's pages. They chanted in unison, barely needing to read from the book because they knew nearly ever spell. The baby turned and kicked in her belly. She moved a hand to calm him, never missing a beat in their chanting.

"O spirits, work my will. We ask for protection from Sebastian Caldecott." Nahla shouted, as the wind in the room strengthened and howled.

Gilda paused in her chanting to echo Nahla's request. She frowned, focusing her gaze on her daughter's belly. "I think we have a little help. I'm sensing quite a bit of powerful energy from the baby. He's already stronger than the average infant warlock."

Nahla nodded. "I feel his energy, too. I sense he's afraid and confused."

Two of the candles flickered out, only to reignite on their own moments later. Mother and daughter shared a grim expression. The spirits were trying to relay a message and it was a dark one. They began chanting again, despite the sinking feeling in Nahla's gut. She repeated her request.

A ghostly voice filled the room. "What is dead should

Sebastian's image appeared in the center of the witches' circle and disappeared just as quickly. All the lit candles were snuffed out by unseen hands and the wind died.

Gilda gripped Nahla's hands. "There's something even dark about Sebastian we don't know. The spirits are clearly hupset. We need to move you to the Underground quickly.

Nahla gave her a tremulous smile. "I only hope this spell will hold long enough for me to have this baby in peace. I know about Sebastian's dark side, but not everything. I can't make sense of what the spirit was trying to tell us.

Nahla gave her a tremulous smile. "I only hope this spell will hold long enough for me to have this baby in peace. I know about Sebastian's dark side, but not everything. I can't make any sense of what the spirit was trying to tell us."

Gilda stroked her cheek. "Trust in the magick, honey. The spirits have always stood with us. They'll make themselves understood soon enough."

Across the city in their townhome, Sebastian stared at the closet in disbelief. All he could see were empty hangers and poles. Nahla had cleared out most of her personal things and left her wedding rings on the bed. He shoved the door closed in a rage. She had left him, and worse, taken his unborn son. He knew she intended to cut him out of their lives. She had no idea who she was dealing with if she thought he would simply accept this.

Sebastian clapped his hands together, creating a small ball of fire. He opened his palms, carefully watching the flames. Just as Nahla's image came into focus, the fire died. He stumbled, clutching his forehead. The spirits at work protecting Nahla were draining his power. "Fuck," he muttered. A framed picture of the two of them went flying against a wall, the glass shattering. There had to be a magick workaround to locate her beacon. Patience had never been his strong suit, but he would wait for just the right time to try his magick again.

THREE

Kauai, Hawaii – One Month Later

NAHLA WRIGGLED HER TOES IN THE FINE GRAINS OF SAND, breathing in deeply. She took a step forward into the foamy wave, delighting in the cold. The late afternoon sun's rays were still plenty warm as they bathed the whole beach in shades of gold and red. Here she was, safely hidden by the Hawaiian chapter of Spellbound Underground, and her soul rejoiced at the freedom.

She had even put on her daring black bikini, something she had abandoned wearing since being with Sebastian. He would've hated seeing her lush, rounded breasts and ripening pregnant belly on display. Her lips curved into an impish smile as she caught the appreciative gaze of another male passerby on the beach. He walked on and she focused her attention on the cabana where her things were. Perhaps it was time for a virgin margarita with a basket of salsa and chips.

She grabbed up her bag and flip flop sandals from the

cabana and headed toward the steps that lead to the back lobby entrance of the Jade Resort, where she was staying. The breeze nearly sent her sun hat flying as she entered the hotel and she caught it with a quick hand, pushing it firmly on her head.

Nahla greeted the afternoon desk clerk on her way to the staircase and he nodded with a warm smile. She grimaced as she bypassed the elevators. *No thanks...* It was no big deal to take the stairs up to the third floor. At her door, she slid in the key card and entered her spacious room. She tossed her beach bag on a plush white chair and headed to the luxurious bathroom, done in granite and sanded wood. She wanted nothing more in the moment than to stand under the warm jets of water and talk to her baby. He seemed to like that.

Stripping down quickly, Nahla was soon in the shower, watching the water droplets spray her belly. As she sang a lilting island tune she had picked up from the natives, she caressed her bump. She was rewarded with light movement from within and a smile curved her lips. She had first felt her unborn son move a few weeks ago. Her mother's joy was tinged with sadness that she had no one near to share it with. Telling her mom over the phone wasn't quite the same.

After her shower, she put on a flirty white sundress and strappy sandals. The chips and salsa beckoned so she quickly tossed a few items into her purse and headed downstairs to the in-resort restaurant, a rowdy tourist spot named The Wicked Chicken.

She entered through the bar portion of the place and her gaze immediately settled on a familiar native of the island and bartender. "Joseph!"

The young man in the island floral shirt turned around

and he flashed her a brilliant white smile, a nice contrast to his bronze skin. "Greetings, Nahla!" He pointed at an open seat at the bar and she made herself comfortable on the bar stool. He wiped down the area with a towel. "Did you catch some sun and waves today?"

She nodded. "I haven't missed a day since I arrived here. Dinner's not for a while, but I'm craving chips and salsa."

"Would you like that with a virgin margarita?"

"Most definitely."

He soon set the basket of warm chips and a small jar of salsa in front of her. She closed her eyes with a small moan as she set about devouring the appetizer. They made small talk between him serving other customers, mostly rambunctious college age kids. Finally, as the crowd dispersed to other parts of the restaurant, Joseph rested his forearms on the bar in front of her.

He leaned in, speaking soft enough for only her ears to hear. "I hope the Underground hasn't let you down?"

Nahla smiled, clutching his hand. "Are you kidding me? This is a paradise I never imagined. The Underground has tended to my every need and kept me safe. I thank you and your coven family."

Joseph gave her hand a squeeze. "And we're happy to do it. No woman, witch or otherwise, deserves abuse at the hands of a man who claims to love her."

He stepped away to serve another customer and Nahla's gaze drifted around the bar. She sipped her margarita, tapping her feet to the salsa rhythm pounding from the speakers. It was good to finally be at peace, hundreds of miles away from Sebastian and his dark drama. She would deal with him again when she was in a better bargaining position.

Her gaze was caught by a tall, well-built man looking

inside the restaurant from the patio. Dread settled like a heavy stone in her belly and she stopped mid chew. She would know that long blond hair whipping in the breeze anywhere. Dear God, he had found her in her island paradise.

She realized after a few tense moments that she could see through the figure at the window. Sebastian's specter was ephemeral and already beginning to fade. He was using his magick's eyes to search for her and could still be hundreds of miles away. She kept her face averted and, when she looked back, the figure was gone.

Nahla frantically waved a hand to catch Joseph's attention. He came to her, his brows furrowed in concern. "What's wrong?"

She pointed at the large window. "I just saw Sebastian's specter outside. Despite all of my concealment spells, he's tracking me." She grabbed up her bag and hopped off the stool. "I need the Underground to move me ASAP."

Joseph removed his bartender apron and came around the bar to her side. "I'll alert my mother and the coven. Before we move you, we need to strengthen the magick around you. Come on—let's get you out of here to a safe place."

He grasped her hand and led her out the bar through the back entrance.

Two hours later at dusk, after a flurry of preparations, Nahla sat in the back of a small car headed for the airport. It struck her with a twinge of regret that her last memory of her island paradise was Joseph putting her in the car with a sad smile, despite his words of comfort. She tightly clutched a ticket for a flight headed to Vermont. Part of her was already resigned to a messy confrontation with Sebastian and she heaved a deep sigh, resting her head on the seat. *But, what if we've outsmarted him...*

Anger simmered in her gut at the fact that she should even be in this situation, pregnant and vulnerable. Now was not the time to fight with him—that would come soon enough after the baby was born. It was best to stay hidden and maintain her freedom, for now. She rubbed her belly. "We're off on another adventure, baby."

———

Nahla stood in the baggage area of the airport, her large blue suitcase next to her. Bustling crowds of travelers made their way around her as she searched the sea of signs, looking for her name. She had arrived well-rested after the long flight to Burlington, Vermont, but was still eager to settle in and relax at the Autumn Moon Inn.

After a few minutes, she spotted her name written in bright red ink on a sign held by a young man with long brown hair, wearing a white oxford shirt. She smiled slightly, waving to him, and moved her suitcase in his direction. He approached her with a broad grin, and she noted the tag on his shirt read "Peter".

He immediately took hold of the suitcase handle. "Hello, Ms. Gregory. I'm the shuttle driver for the Autumn Moon Inn. Name's Peter. I hope your flight was good?"

She nodded, thanking him. "They supplied me with plenty of snacks."

"We'll just walk across to the parking lot and I'll have you loaded up in the shuttle in no time."

She followed him outside the downstairs exit doors and stepped into the bright sunlight. A warm, gentle breeze ruffled her hair as she kept pace with him across the lot. Every airport looked the same so she was excited to get on the road to see more of the area. They soon reached the small shuttle and Peter helped her in, before loading up her suitcase.

Nahla bit back a hundred questions as the driver smoothly guided the shuttle bus in and around traffic. Finally, her curiosity got the better of her. "How long will this perfect weather last here?"

Peter chuckled, glancing over at her for a moment. "Oh, it won't be long before October's here, bringing the rainy days with it. Will you still be our guest during the Halloween Festival? We have one every year."

"Sounds like fun. Yes, I plan to be at the inn for a while."

After a brief conversation about the town of Catnip, they settled into a comfortable silence. Once they left the downtown area of Burlington, she focused her attention on the large trees that lined the side of the highway as they sped along. The lush, green leaves were starting to give way to majestic shades of gold and red.

As he had promised, the ride into Catnip hadn't been overly long and she perked up when she saw the Autumn Moon Inn sign for the next highway exit. She marveled at the charm of the small town as they traveled the back roads. Small cottages and office buildings lined the streets, with even more trees in their seasonal glory fusion of vivid colors. Catnip was as postcard perfect as they came.

Peter soon pulled the shuttle bus to a stop in front of a white mansion with a gorgeous wraparound porch. He looked back at her with a smile. "I got you here, safe and sound."

Nahla stepped down off the shuttle and looked around with a touch of wonder. This was so far removed from the crowded, bustling city of Los Angeles. She already had a good feeling about being here. Peter unloaded her suitcase and led the way inside the inn. The leaves crunched beneath her feet.

Once inside, she took in the antique furniture, set off with colorful crotched pillows. The entrance parlor displayed overstuffed chairs and decorative mahogany end tables. Dark wood floors stretched out ahead of her. She followed Peter to the front desk, where a teenage clerk with long dark hair stood with a welcoming smile.

"Here's Ms. Gregory, Samantha. Can you please let Drew know she's here?" Peter nodded his head in the upstairs direction.

"Welcome to the Autumn Moon Inn, Ms. Gregory." She gestured with a hand. "Actually, Drew is right here to greet you."

Nahla turned to see a tall, well-built man with chestnut colored hair approaching. He extended a hand and she shook it firmly. "I'm happy you're here to stay with us for a while. I'm Drew Winchester, the owner."

Nahla's lips curved upward. "It's a pleasure to meet you and be here, Mr. Winchester."

He waved a hand. "I'm just Drew."

"And, I'm just Nahla."

He nodded, clearing his throat. "I'll let Samantha get you checked in and settled into your room. In the meantime, you should know that your contact person here in Catnip is Tomas Castillo. He lives in town, not too far away. He requested to meet you here in the solarium, as soon as you arrived." He pointed toward the rear of the parlor. "The solarium has actually been remodeled into our Cat's Paw Café."

Nahla looked in that direction, noting the theme was continued with crotched tablecloths, crimson walls, and the same dark wood flooring. One wall was glass, offering a breathtaking view of the outdoors. "That sounds completely charming."

"I'll give Tomas a call to let him know you've arrived." With a smile, Drew disappeared back into the room he had come from. She thanked a departing Peter and turned her attention back to Samantha.

Tomas scrolled the text messages on his cell phone, searching for one in particular. He had just heard from Drew Winchester. His witch ward, Nahla Gregory, was here. His gaze lighted on the message with her picture and brief information about her situation. He frowned, sliding his phone back in his pants pocket. An abusive warlock was serious business and he was determined to treat it as such. His job as a host for Spellbound Underground was to keep his wards safe and he had never failed in that task.

He patted his pants pockets and let out a grunt of frustration. No keys. He looked around and found them on the small kitchen table. His cottage was small and humble but decoratively charming and comfortable. Nahla Gregory was an L.A. girl but he hoped she would be impressed with his home and the quaint little town of Catnip. He didn't need city-girl attitude.

That set him on the path of thinking about the last woman he had let into his life, a city-girl witch, who swiftly lost interest in him once she knew his darkest secret. It hurt but it made sense. Most young witches were drawn to a more powerful warlock, preferably with a family trust fund. Tomas knew he was lacking in both areas. He had come to accept this as a part of his life.

Locking down the house, he set off in his car. It was, at most, a fifteen minute drive to the inn. Traffic was rarely a problem and he soon arrived, parking in front. He headed through the massive oak doors and approached the front desk. He idly tapped his fingers on it and waited a few moments. Samantha appeared from the back room and greeted him.

The clerk pointed in the direction of the café in the rear. "Ms. Gregory is already waiting for you."

He smiled and thanked her, before moving toward the solarium. There was a fair number of customers seated but he spotted her almost immediately. Nahla Gregory was a natural standout in any crowd. He observed her for a moment as she sipped from a coffee cup. Petite, with a beautiful face, brown skin, and a mass of wildly curly dark hair, he could easily picture her as the victim of an abusive lover.

Their eyes met and his heart caught in his chest. Her smile was tremulous, and he knew right then he would do his absolute best to shelter her from her own personal storm. Damn Sebastian Caldecott for hurting her. He strode over to her table, giving her a gentle smile.

"Hi Nahla." He caught her small hand in his grasp, enjoying the soft skin and faint fragrance of scented lotion. "I'm Tomas Castillo." He nervously cleared his throat and sat down across from her. "From Spellbound Underground. I'm here to help you."

Her words were blunt. "Great, because I need all the help I can get. My ex was searching for me in Kauai and I'm desperate to make sure that doesn't happen again."

She moved around in her chair and his attention focused on her belly. His confusion cleared after a moment. "Forgive me, but I see you're clearly...pregnant. Your mother told me there were two of you and I expected a toddler. The energy your little one is giving off is very strong."

Nahla's expression was rueful. "My son clearly gets that

from his biological father. Sebastian, my soon-to-be ex-husband, is an extremely powerful warlock."

Tomas held her gaze and impulsively took her hand in his. He wasn't going to mince his words. "You're freer than you realize, Nahla. Sebastian Caldecott is already married. Your marriage to him is invalid and not legally binding."

FOUR

HER MOUTH GAPED OPEN AND SHE LOOKED ABSOLUTELY dumbstruck. "What?"

Tomas reached for his phone, murmuring his disgust in Spanish. He tapped the screen, pulling up an email and set it in front of her. "I've had an investigator from the Witches Council working on your case since I first heard from your mother. His results are right here."

Tomas watched her delicate hands tremble as she read the email and he was overwhelmed with pity and deep anger.

Nahla clasped her hands together tightly as she read the damning report, line by line. She willed herself not to give into the memories that had her stomach in knots. She was already deeply bonded with her unborn son and perhaps he sensed something was wrong as his tiny limbs poked her. She rubbed a soothing, protective hand over her belly.

By the time she finished reading, her blood was boiling. She looked up, meeting Tomas' soulful brown eyes, grateful beyond words. "Thank you for this. For everything." Her voice croaked with emotion. "I did this. I shouldn't have allowed myself to get caught up in Sebastian's twisted world. Ten years. The bastard's been married for ten, long years." She handed the phone back.

"I'm sure you're devastated and—"

Nahla shook her head slowly in denial. "No. Devastation would indicate some level of love leftover. I'm tired of crying over him and I'm relieved to be free."

A gentle smile creased Tomas' handsome face. "But? There's usually a "but" in situations like this."

"Damn right. I'm furious at being played for a fool." She raised a hand. "I don't want revenge, though I could go for the jugular. I just want to have my baby in peace. Can you and Spellbound Underground help me with that?"

He nodded. "You can stay with me here in Catnip as long as you need to after the baby is born. When the time comes for the birth, I can arrange for it all to be handled with the utmost care and discretion. I can help you rebuild your life, Nahla."

Relief coursed through her and she relaxed in the chair. Her and her baby were a package deal that she was afraid Tomas wouldn't be able to accept. But instead, he was offering her a safe haven. She silently whispered a prayer of thanks, her lips curving in a smile. "Thank you, Tomas. I really appreciate it."

He cleared his throat. "Of course." He gestured at the coffee cup. "If you're finished, I'd like to take you somewhere in town. It'll be fun and give you a break from all this."

"That sounds like just what I need." She grabbed up her small handbag. "I'll settle the bill."

He pulled his wallet from his pocket, tossing a few dollar bills onto the table. "Don't worry about that."

"You don't have to pay my way. I'm just a little low on cash, not destitute."

Sliding his hand around her arm, he helped her stand. He spoke close to her ear. "You're my ward and I'm sworn to take care of you. I won't let you down."

A shiver of delight tingled her spine at his low spoken words. She quickly dismissed it. He was a beautiful man to look at with that dark hair falling carelessly into his eyes, two dark brown pools of raw expression. He was attractive—end of story.

Later, they pulled up in front of a little white cottage in Tomas' car. Nahla enjoyed every moment of the ride there, paying close attention to the quiet beauty of every building they had passed traveling through the town.

He flipped off his seatbelt. "Her name is Daureen and she's very friendly. She'll be thrilled to help you."

She frowned in confusion. "Help me?"

Tomas grinned. "She reads tarot cards."

Nahla snorted. "I'm sure this will be the darkest reading she's ever given."

He stepped out of the car and came around to her side, opening the door. "Fun, remember?"

The front door opened to reveal an elderly woman in a black dress, her silver hair pinned up in an elegant bun. She welcomed them inside with a smile. "Hello. I'm Daureen. And who are you, dear?"

Nahla shook her hand. "I'm Nahla Gregory. It's nice to meet you."

Daureen nodded, turning to Tomas. "Is she one of yours?"

"Yes, she's my new ward. We just came for a tarot reading."

"The baby's just fine." Daureen's eyes gleamed with mischief.

Nahla's laugh tinkled, feeling the weight of her problems lift a bit. She immediately liked the older woman. They followed her from the front room to another room in the rear of the small house. A deck of tarot cards was set on a small wood table with a few matching chairs around it. They all sat down, with Nahla directly across from the elderly woman.

"Tap the card deck with your fingertips, dear."

Nahla lightly stroked the cards and Daureen began spreading them out. She frowned deeply for a moment as she turned one card over. By the second card, Nahla's heart began to sink.

"How bad is it?" she asked nervously.

Daureen harrumphed. "Bad. That dark cloud following you is pervasive. Evil always is." She turned over the third card and her face brightened. "However, the universe always finds a way to bless the strong. Your inner strength will guide and sustain you, Nahla. And, you're not alone. This is Tomas' fight, too."

He raised his eyebrows. "My fight?"

The older woman patted his hand. "It will soon make sense. Let's continue."

She turned over another card and met Nahla's anxious gaze. "The spirits have a message for you. What is dead should remain dead."

Nahla's pulse raced. "I've heard that before,' she murmured. "Can you tell me what it means?"

Daureen gave her a gentle smile. "The spirits are being very tight-lipped right now. My best guess is that they will reveal everything you need to know when you need to know it."

Later on the drive back to the inn, Nahla mulled over Daureen's words. The doom and gloom with a positive outcome was expected but Tomas' involvement in her situation was definitely not. This was her fight and she didn't expect him to be a part of her madness. She was his ward and nothing else. *But…what if?*

She turned her gaze from the scenery whizzing by to study his profile as he sat behind the wheel. Classically handsome with to die for eyes, she noted. He was strong but there was something askew with his aura. She sensed a fragility of spirit in him, as if he'd been broken. He gave her a quick smile before turning his attention back to the road. She looked away, feeling guilty. The last thing they both needed was her attraction to him messing things up.

They pulled up to the inn and Tomas was quick to open her door. He followed her up the steps to the front doors. She stopped, turning to face him. "Thank you for the tarot reading. Instead of upsetting me, I feel calm now that I know the spirits are on my side. Plus, it was fun"

He inclined his head. "Well, I did promise you that. I'm sure you're tired from your plane ride so I'll let you rest. How about I pick you up tomorrow morning at ten and, after breakfast, I'll show you my home. It's not far from here."

Nahla smiled. "Sure. I'd love that."

"Great. I'll text you in the morning when I'm on my way." He cleared his throat. "I'll do everything I can to protect you."

Without another word or backward glance, he headed down the steps and got in his car. She watched him pull away before she entered the inn, her thoughts dark once again. She was beginning to feel that Tomas Castillo was a wild card. He seemed steady and dependable but the shadows in his eyes told another story.

Sebastian cursed loudly, pounding his fist on the heavy oak desk. He had spent the greater part of the afternoon locked in his study, trying spell after spell but he couldn't locate Nahla and his son. The ungrateful bitch had help in disappearing. Her mother abruptly hung up every time he called, and he was absolutely sure she knew exactly where they were.

His magick never failed him. Ever. He allowed his rage and frustration to settle before thinking of it again as a challenge. He would eventually put all the puzzle pieces together and, when he did, there would be hell to pay for all parties involved. He smiled darkly, imagining Nahla cowering in fear when he finally confronted her.

She would eventually use her magick in such a way that would allow him to track her again. Her aura normally flashed as a beacon, but she had dampened it, somehow. All he needed was one slip-up and he'd be on her trail. Oh yes, he'd find her. She had a lot of treachery to answer for.

Sebastian glanced at the clock and grabbed up his cell phone. He keyed in a familiar number and waited as it rang a few times. "Sebastian. I've been waiting all day for your call. Are you coming home tonight?"

His voice took on a calm and soothing tone. "Hello, Catherine. I'm sorry I'm so late in calling you. I've been tied up in meetings here in L.A. all afternoon. I'm not flying home tonight, regretfully. I have to catch a flight in the morning to Alaska to secure an important business deal."

She sighed deeply. "Any other woman would think you were cheating, but I know you better than that, my loving husband. So...when can I expect you back here in New York?"

He chuckled. "Certainly by next weekend, my love."

They chatted for several moments before he ended the call, with a promise to call again when he reached Alaska. He leaned back in the leather chair, absently swirling the ice in his glass of vodka. He hadn't really lied—he did have a business deal to handle in Alaska, but it was nobody's business but his. His wife, both wives, would never know the true nature of the things he made happen every day. His thoughts turned to Nahla and his baby and his lips upturned in a grim smile. He had a good feeling that the whole situation with her would turn in his favor once he met with his associate in Anchorage.

He was almost certain he had picked up her trail in Kauai, but he couldn't be sure because her faint beacon had simply vanished. He acknowledged that she may have been using a spell to throw him off and had never been there at all. He clapped his hands together and a small ball of crimson fire formed between them. He focused his energy for long moments and, again, saw nothing. He grunted in frustration as the ball disappeared and sipped deeply from his glass.

———

"This my humble home," Tomas said, pride evident in his voice.

Nahla stepped inside from the charming front porch, all done in sanded wood. The house was even more impressive, and she looked around, taking in the hardwood floors, arched doorways that led to other parts of the small house, and crème walls. She turned to find his eyes on her and was pleased at the warmth she saw in them, feeling admired in her blue maxi dress even though she was as round as could be.

"Tomas, you have a beautiful home," she exclaimed.

He nodded, closing the heavy wood front door. "Thank you. I have invested a lot in this place. It's small but so are my needs."

Nahla was about to comment when a small bundle with blonde ponytails and a yellow sundress emerged from the back hallway and launched herself at Tomas with an excited whoop. "Mr. Tomas! I've been waiting all morning for you."

He picked her up with a welcoming grin. "Good morning, Mina. Where's your mom?"

"Trying to get someone to calm down. She's been hyper all morning."

Nahla turned her gaze to a waif like blonde coming from the back. Her heart dropped like a sack of stones. Of course, Tomas had a pretty girlfriend. And she was apparently sharing his home with her child. She mustered a smile at the woman.

"Nahla, this is Lisbeth and her daughter, Mina. They're also my wards, just like you."

The weight in her chest lifted slightly. Ok, this wasn't so bad. "Oh. So they live—"

Lisbeth extended a hand and she shook it. "Yes, we're only living here temporarily until the, um, threat in our lives is gone. Mina, this is Ms. Nahla. Say hello."

The little girl waved. "Hello, Ms. Nahla."

Her lips curved upwards. "Nice to meet you, Mina."

Tomas lowered her to the floor. "They're in a similar situation to yours, Nahla."

Lisbeth spoke gently. "It's nice to have you here. We

expected a baby with you but not one you're still carrying." She gestured at her belly bump.

Nahla laughed. "Yes, Tomas explained that to me. I'm about four months in."

Tomas turned his gaze to her. "I had an idea in mind when I brought you here. Spellbound Underground has always been a labor of love that my mom was devoted to when she was alive. I know you're not destitute but—"

She held up a hand. "I'm not."

"But, there's only so much money allotted to each witch ward. Lisbeth cleans my home and cooks the meals for us. I pay her out of my own pocket. I can do the same for you if you're willing to do some light filing and bookkeeping for me." His voice was gentle.

Her mind was made up in two seconds flat. "Yes. I'd like that."

"Great. I can show you my office and explain everything to you right now."

Lisbeth guided the little girl towards the back hallway. "We would like to go into town with you this morning, if you don't mind dropping us off and picking us up after your shift."

As they discussed the details, Nahla focused on her small victory. She now had a job to keep her occupied and to supplement the money she had when she'd started this journey to freedom. It was enough to help her begin a new life for her and her baby. She again felt an overwhelming sense of gratitude for Tomas and all the other witches of Spellbound Underground.

He beckoned to her and she followed him down the back hallway. As they entered his office, Lisbeth gave her a goodbye wave and disappeared into one of the rooms with Mina. She came to stand next to a large desk, every inch covered with papers.

His tone was rueful. "As you can see, I'm a little behind on organizing things. I'm hoping you can fix this mess."

"You've called on the right person to help you out. I'm an administrative assistant in addition to a graduate student." She frowned for a moment. "Or, at least I was."

"Soon, you'll be able to reclaim your life, Nahla. I'll do what I have to do to ensure that."

She whispered a thank you, fighting tears. How had she lost herself so completely in Sebastian's mad lifestyle?

Tomas showed her around his office, explaining things to her. Midway, a question burned as curiosity got the better of her. "So, how on earth do you support yourself?"

"I'm a mental health counselor. I work a few days a week here at the clinic in town and I make the drive to Burlington once a week to counsel patients at the hospital. I make a pretty good living and I have a job I always dreamed about."

Nahla nodded. "That job suits you. You're everything a counselor should be—honest, genuinely caring."

Tomas shrugged lightly. "Gifts from my mom, I suppose. She taught me that showing honest care and concern for others matters far more than any paycheck."

"That's a refreshing change to see in a man. All Sebastian truly cared about was money and appearances."

He went quiet for a moment, assessing her. "How on earth did you ever end up with him? Later, I intend to find all that out as well as give you some history about Spellbound Underground." He pulled his keys from his pants pocket. "For now, I'll leave you here to get situated and figure out your own filing system. I'm off to the clinic in town. See you in a few hours."

Tomas patted her shoulder and headed down the hallway. She heard the door close, as he left with Lisbeth and a chattering Mina. Nahla sucked in a deep breath. Though his words were kind, they still stung. She agreed—how in hell had she ended up essentially being Sebastian's toy when he got bored? Her parents had raised her to be self-sufficient and, as a result, the adult her was fiercely independent. She had taken her eye off the ball and become his sucker, falling for his act of care and concern for her welfare.

She began organizing the tumble of papers on the desk. There was no time for feeling sorry for herself. She had to now consider the welfare of her young one. An hour passed before curiosity set in, once again. She speculatively looked across the room at the closet. Did he keep his tools for magick in there? Most witches she knew did. She longed to know more about the mysterious Tomas, and this seemed a good way to do it. She moved to the door, her hand lingering on the doorknob. *Should I...?* She turned it and peered inside. *Paydirt.*

The closet held tons of jars and small bags, all filled with things familiar to every witch for spellcasting. She looked up at the midnight blue warlock hat on a hook, decorated with moons and stars, smiling. There was that wonderful whimsy that sometimes surfaced when she was around Tomas.

It occurred to her after a moment that this would be the perfect time to reinforce the cloaking spell that she cast to protect her from Sebastian. She slid the warlock hat on her head. She needed all the good luck she could get and Tomas seemed pretty lucky. Setting up her witches' circle took little time and soon she was seated in the middle, sprinkling various powders all around her as she chanted. A small wind picked up in the room, despite the closed windows. Her smile was serene. The spirits were answering her request with good fortune.

———

"You did a fantastic job of arranging my office. Thank you."

Nahla gave Tomas a bright smile. "Well, you're paying me good money. I'll do the best I can."

They sat across from each other at a small table in the Cat's Paw Café. Tomas had returned home a few hours later, as promised, and brought her back to the inn for an early dinner. She pushed her empty plate to the side.

"You promised to tell me all about the origins of Spellbound Underground."

Tomas nodded. "My family's part of the story begins with my great-grandmother, Rosario. She was a witch with as much power as her heart was big. Unfortunately, she was a softie with the wrong man, a normal man. He seduced her, taking advantage of her goodness. Once he got what he wanted from her, he spread the word that she believed she was an actual witch to several townspeople and the police in a bid to have her committed."

He smiled gently at Nahla's look of horror. "He was married and would've done anything to keep Rosario from telling anybody about their affair. She cast a spell, asking the spirits to save her, and it cost the man his life. She lived with the guilt until the day she died. She wanted to create a safe haven for other witches who were in trouble and so, Spellbound Underground was born..."

She listened intently as his softly spoken words weaved a tale of dark magick and intrigue surrounding the creation of the organization a hundred years ago. She had a thousand questions, biting them back to not miss a word he said. Long minutes later, he finished speaking, looking at her expectantly.

"It's amazing. Your great-grandmother was a founding member of Spellbound, even at great personal risk to her life. Those were dangerous times to be a witch. No wonder this is all so personal to you. You're a part of her legacy."

Tomas' smile was faint. "Not that it does me any good."

Nahla frowned. "I don't understand…"

He sipped from the coffee cup and set it down. His expressive eyes flashed with anguish. "My magick is gone, Nahla."

FIVE

"WHAT DO YOU MEAN BY...GONE?"

He heaved a deep sigh. "My father was a lot like Sebastian. Domineering and abusive, to both my mom and me. The trauma, I guess, was too great for a kid to handle and my mind suppressed my abilities. I'm like a dead wall outlet. I can still sense some things but not much beyond that."

Nahla covered his hand with hers. "Oh, Tomas. This must be torturous for you. I can't imagine going a whole day without casting some kind of spell. The things we take for granted."

He squeezed her hand tightly for a moment. "I miss my magick but I've managed without it. I've learned to focus on my other, less extraordinary talents and I live a good life." His gaze moved downward. "I want the same for you and your precious cargo."

She sensed his deep sadness and decided not to push any further. She knew him well enough now to know he didn't want or need her pity. Pressing on would only make him feel as if she felt nothing but sorry for him and that was far from the truth. She was beginning to feel connected to him, though it would only complicate things.

They chatted briefly before he saw her safely to her room upstairs. At her door, he gave her a pickup time for tomorrow and a chaste kiss on the cheek. His warm soft lips on her skin sent tingles down her spine that remained long after he wished her a good evening and headed down the hallway.

Later, she tossed and turned in bed, trying to find a comfortable position to accommodate her growing belly. The baby was also restless, poking her with strong limbs. She couldn't stop thinking about Tomas's goodness. Finally, she gave up trying to sleep with her thoughts tumbling. She hadn't said all she wanted to say. She grabbed her cell phone from the nightstand.

Nahla put her thoughts into a simple, concise text message to Tomas. She ended it with the words, "You are more than your magick."

Just as she placed the cell on the nightstand to charge, her phone chimed a response from him. "Bless you and your kind heart, Nahla. Your words mean a lot to me. I'm bent but not broken. Aren't we all, though? Sleep tight."

She stretched out on the bed, a smile curving her lips. She was playing with fire but at least she wasn't dancing with the devil anymore. That's all Sebastian would ever be, a devil. No matter how it complicated things, she was definitely falling for the right kind of guy, now. The timing sucked, but when was everything ever perfect? She wasn't going to wait for all the right stars to align in the heavens. With that comforting thought and the little one in her belly finally still, she drifted off.

Across town, Tomas tossed fitfully, trying to find a comfortable position. His body ached and not from his evening run. He wanted her. Nahla had him stiff below the waist and, now alone in the dark with his thoughts, he acknowledged the spark between them wasn't in his imagination. He had seen the desire in her eyes earlier at his house, though she tried to mask it, as he was, behind the veil of budding friendship.

Nahla was beautiful in more than a physical sense. Having gotten to know her over the past few days, he was struck by her strength of character and her resilience. Her ex- lover and the situation hadn't destroyed her faith in the goodness of humanity. Instead of bitterness, she glowed with charming optimism in the future for her and her baby.

He thought about the Witches Council's firm stance about involving oneself in the relationship between a warlock and his witch. While it was true that Sebastian was already married to another witch, Nahla still carried his child. How would the Council view that? Also, he acknowledged that he was virtually powerless against the far more powerful warlock. Tomas had his doubts that Caldecott would simply let this go if he found out where Nahla was and how she came to be there.

Tomas groaned loudly. She was pregnant with another warlock's child, yet he burned for her. *Let her come to you...* He punched his pillow in good, old fashioned sexual frustration, resolve setting in. He would let her find her way into his bed...but only if she didn't take too long.

———

"Tomas? Are you listening?" Nahla waved a hand in front of his face.

Snapped out of his thoughts and gave her a smile. He had been distracted by her lush body in a simple, colorful dress and her delicious, ripe lips all morning. They stood in his home office and she held a document file in her outstretched hand. He took it from her and made a show of studying the pages, though his head was still miles away.

"Yes," he murmured distractedly. "This file is perfect. You can put it in the outgoing box."

She nodded and, to his relief, turned away. His body was tensed. His erection at ten thirty in the morning, while they worked together was something he definitely didn't want her to notice. He put space between them, feigning looking for something on his desk.

Her soft voice purred behind him. "I meant what I said last night in my text. You really are more than your blocked magick, Tomas."

His back stiffened. "Then why do I feel neutered? What kind of warlock can't use his magick?" His voice was gruff.

Nahla placed a gentle hand on his shoulder. "A warlock who needs help. My help, if you let me. If we can get to the source of your problem—"

"My problem is psychological trauma from a father who beat me for nothing and knocked my mother around for fun. My power has been gone since I was a teen and I seriously doubt there's anything you can do to bring it back."

Unexpectedly, he felt Nahla's arms around him from behind. "I'm so sorry," she said softly. He let her hold him because it felt damn good to be in her embrace. After long moments, he turned to her and held her tightly. He murmured a few words in Spanish in her ear, kissing the shell gently.

Cupping her face in his hands, his lips traveled from her ear to her parted mouth. She didn't respond as if he'd surprised her, instead yielding to him and his rough kiss. His tongue stroked hers as he tasted her sweet for the first time. Trembling against him, she encircled his neck with her arms. Her swollen belly bumped up against his hard cock, but she didn't break the kiss to protest. His secret was out now but she hadn't rejected him.

After long moments of his tongue brushing hers, they broke apart with labored breaths. He put his back to her to hide the deep emotion he was sure was written on his face. Nahla Gregory was under his skin in a way no woman ever had been.

"Wow. That was…even better than I expected."

He faced her suddenly. "That's what I'm thinking, too. But we don't need this complication, Nahla. You have enough to worry about without me making sexual

demands—"

Her laughter tinkled in the silence. "Your "demands" are more than welcome, though I agree about the timing. It sucks."

He nodded solemnly. "Let's table this discussion until dinner at the inn tonight. If we continue, um, kissing, we may end up in my bedroom doing a lot more than that."

Her smile was breathtaking. "I concur, though making out with my boss was fun."

Tomas laughed heartily. His spirit felt lighter than it had in a long time and this runaway witch was to blame.

Tomas brought the car to a smooth stop in a parking spot and gave Nahla a quick glance.

"So, this is Burlington," she said, gazing through the windshield at the majestic trees that formed a canopy above the entrance to the large hospital where he worked.

He nodded. "I only need to grab a stack of files and then we can head back home." He flung off the seat belt. "Thanks for coming with me today."

Nahla touched his arm. "I admit I'm curious to see your other office. Is it as disorganized as your one at home was?" She offered him a teasing smile.

Tomas chuckled. "Worse." He shut his door and came around to open hers.

As they entered the hospital, the bustling sights and sounds assailed her. Nurses in their blue scrubs rushed by them. Tomas left her standing alone for a few moments. He returned with a visitor pass and she placed the sticky badge on her chest. As he led her to the elevators, she froze in place. He stopped to look at her.

Nahla licked her lips with her suddenly dry tongue. "Um...what floor is your office on?" Her words came out as a squeak.

Tomas looked at her strangely. "Fourth floor. Why?" He moved to push the up button.

Like a trapped animal, she began searching around the lobby for her usual escape route. She heaved a sigh of relief when she spotted the entrance to the stairs. She spoke without meeting his gaze. "I don't...don't do so well in elevators."

The concern in his tone was evident. "Motion sickness because of the baby?"

She nodded, backing away as the doors slid open and he stepped inside. "Something like that. Um...I'll meet you on the fourth floor. I'm taking the stairs."

He held out his hand to her. "That's more work than

necessary. Come on, Nahla. It only takes a few seconds to get there."

She put her back to him. calling out over her shoulder. "That's a few seconds too long." She hurried to the stairs entrance, praying it wasn't locked. She turned the knob and entered the stairwell. Her heart raced and it was hard to swallow with her mouth drying out. Hands trembling, she gripped the handrail. Up she went, climbing slowly and carefully until she reached the fourth floor.

Tomas was waiting for her at the door. His brows were furrowed as his gaze searched her face. He gently took her arm and led her down the long hallway to his office. "Is your sickness really that severe?" he questioned as he turned his key in the lock.

Nahla had a hard time meeting his eyes, nodding. "Worse than you can imagine." To stifle further questions about it, she quickly brushed past him into his dark office. She definitely wasn't ready to discuss with him, or anyone else, her acquired fear of confined spaces, thanks to Sebastian. She acknowledged that Tomas was probably the perfect person to talk it over with, but she wore her new disorder like a badge of shame.

Tomas flipped on the lights. "Let me grab the files and then we'll take the stairs down."

Nahla murmured a thank you to his back, trying to relax the clenched, nervous fists her hands had become.

Later, on the drive back, Nahla deliberately kept her gaze focused on the scenery whizzing by out the window, not wanting to meet Tomas' frequent gazes at her profile. She felt utterly humiliated by her inability to conquer the fear of confined spaces, like elevators, Sebastian had given her by locking her in the bathroom. Without fail, her heart raced, and she broke out in cold sweats in small spaces. Her head told her Tomas was the perfect person to share her overwhelming fears with, but her heart slammed on the brakes. *It's my problem and one day I'll deal with it…*

She finally turned her gaze to meet Tomas' and saw the concern in his expression. No words were necessary. He obviously knew something was up but wasn't going to push her to speak, thank God. She offered him a tremulous smile and squeezed his free hand.

———

The jet black Audi pulled up to the curb at JFK airport in a steady downpour from the heavens. Sebastian smiled broadly at his wife before opening the rear door and loading his suitcase inside. He slid into the passenger seat of the car, strapping on his seat belt. She leaned over and kissed him lightly before guiding the car into the flow of traffic.

"I see your business deals as a means to an end, a means of maintaining our lifestyle. These trips are monopolizing your time, Sebastian. I'm beginning to think you enjoy them more than you do being at home with me, the boring little wife." Catherine huffed a deep breath as she looked at him quickly.

He could see the clouds of doubt in her eyes. A storm was brewing, and he needed to head it off at the pass. "Catherine, no man would ever refer to you as boring, especially me. My love, these trips are mundane, but necessary. I've been on a lucky streak and I need to work harder than ever to keep winning." He ran a few strands of her long blonde hair through his fingers and kissed her neck. "You love our home and these luxury cars, don't you?"

THE RUNAWAY WITCH'S KISS

Catherine sighed. "The trappings of a wealthy lifestyle are nothing compared to the bond I share with you, husband. I believe I would happily sacrifice it all to have you at home. With me." She poked his chest.

Sebastian leaned his head back against the head rest, closing his eyes. "You will give up nothing and want for nothing in this life, Catherine. I'm sworn to that."

"You're certain you have nothing to tell me? There's no other woman you're hiding on the side?"

Sebastian kept his eyes closed, appearing calm even as his heart thumped unevenly. Annoyance shot through him at her questions. The last thing he needed was for his wife to catch even a hint of his involvement with Nahla. He pinched the bridge of his nose. "I swear to you, there is no other woman in my life. Even if I had the inclination to have an affair, I simply don't have the time." He met her searching gaze for a moment.

Finally, she shrugged. "So, there is no other woman. Well, there it is." She maneuvered through the traffic, flipping the switch for the windshield wipers to high.

Sebastian relaxed in his seat, closing his eyes again. "Yes," he murmured. "There it is."

Nahla didn't stop to question why it felt right to hold Tomas' hand as they walked the inn's grounds under the black velvet sky, punctuated with a bright moon and glowing white stars. Instead, she entwined her fingers with his as she kept pace beside him. They had enjoyed dinner in the Cat's Paw downstairs before heading out.

She recalled the heat of his gaze as she'd descended the staircase to the lobby, stylishly garbed in a sleeveless black dress with an empire waist. Tomas made her feel sexy when she knew she looked far more ripe and maternal than like a sex siren. No four-inch heels—she had to settle for sensible flats.

"Do you want to tell me about what happened at the hospital today?" he prodded. "You and elevators."

She shook her head in denial. "There's really nothing to tell. Motion sickness, like you said."

He gently took her hand in his. "That was my best guess at the time, but I sense it's more complicated than that."

Nahla heaved a deep sigh. "Far more complicated, but that's a conversation I'd rather not have right now. You know my story, but I know so little about yours." She squeezed his hand. "Please…tell me."

She watched his expression grow stony, his jaw tensing. "I can tell you more about my life as it is now, but I really don't want to get into my relationship with my father, if that's what you mean."

"Where is he now?" Her voice was hushed.

"Blessedly dead."

"And your mom?"

Tomas heaved a sigh. "She's gone, too. And, yes, I'm their only child."

Nahla raised their joined hands and planted a kiss on his knuckle. Her smile was sweet as she heard him draw in a breath. "You're all alone in this world. I can only imagine the pain that must bring."

He stopped walking and turned to her. "Not all alone. I have other members of my coven. I have the Spellbound wards, who I frequently shelter."

The moon cast a sliver of light on his face, but she couldn't see the emotion in those expressive eyes. "But…don't you ever get lonely?"

He chuffed softly. "I'm perfectly lonely, Nahla. That's just my lot in life, I guess."

She moved in closer and released his hand. Gentle fingers rubbed his bristly chin. "You don't have to be, Tomas. At least, while I'm here."

His tone was gruff. "Are you inviting me into your bed, sweet Nahla?"

SIX

She wrapped her arms around his neck and let her tentative kiss do the talking. He devoured her mouth, just as he had done before, and his hands stroked her lush ass. They remained lost in each other for long, passionate moments before he broke away, breathing heavily.

"I'm not strong enough to resist you. Is this a spell you cast? Because I feel like, even though we haven't known each other long, I'm drawn to you."

Nahla laughed. "No spell, but I believe we do have a similar vibration that attracts us to each other like magnets. I never felt this connected to Sebastian."

"I asked you if you're inviting me to your room tonight."

"And, I already answered." She headed in the direction of the brightly lit inn. Four seconds. It took Tomas four seconds to catch up with her.

Once upstairs, she unlocked the door to her room, and he followed her inside. She had left the antique lamp on one of her nightstands on and the room glowed dimly. The beige wallpaper with red roses, old wood bed and armoire, and comfortable worn rugs now seemed more romantic than simply quaint. This was the perfect scene to welcome a lover.

She turned to him as he closed the door and leaned back against it, his eyes closed for a moment. Her tentative step toward him was met with his crushing embrace. He covered her mouth with a soulful kiss, his tongue parting her lips to caress hers.

After long moments, Tomas turned her so that her back faced him. Nahla let out heated moans as his warm lips traveled from the shell of her ear down her neck. She didn't protest when he tugged at the strappy ribbon in the back that held the top of her dress together. Clutching his forearm, she whispered words of encouragement as the dress slithered down to the floor, a pool of black at her feet.

Nahla hastily kicked off the flats and faced him, smiling at the burning desire she saw in his eyes. The smile slipped a bit when she remembered she wore a maternity bra and panties. Her hand slid across her swelled belly. "I promise you, I'm not usually this big. And, I do have far sexier taste in undergarments."

Tomas kissed her gently and she felt his body trembling. "You are ripe and full of life. There's no reason to be ashamed of the way you look. It's a pity you can't see yourself as I see you."

He stepped back and shed his clothing, pinning her with his hot gaze. Nahla enjoyed the whole show, especially the part when he stood before her, completely naked. She ran her fingertips across his shoulder blades and leanly muscled arms, drinking him in. She dared to stroke his chest and traced the lines of his abs. At his hiss of breath and eyes narrowed in passion, she paused. She instinctively stepped back, the heat in his gaze singeing her and sending tiny shock waves all over her body. He crooked his finger at her with a lazy smile. "Your turn, baby."

She let him slowly remove her bra and panties without a single protest. It was an unexpected development to no longer feel self-conscious as his hands began to explore her body with strokes of his skilled hands. Soft fingertips traced the lines of her calves and up her thighs. His hands cupped her breasts, caressing the hardened nipples. She sighed as his lips replaced his fingertips, gently suckling each nipple. Her moistening core began to throb with need, and she groaned, placing one of his hands between her thighs.

Tomas responded by sliding his fingers into her damp folds, searching for her hard bud. Nahla cried out when he found it, teasing and rubbing as his lips went again to her nipples. He lifted his head after long moments of torture and backed her toward the bed. He gently stretched her body out and looked down at her.

His voice came out as a whisper. "Bella...bella precioso. My Nahla."

He leaned down, his hands trapping her in on both sides. She thought he meant to kiss her lips but, instead, he planted tiny kisses on her belly. She ached for him in every way in that moment. He was being gentle with both her and her child. She squirmed in need. "Tomas...please..."

His grin was infectious, and she gave him a naughty little smile. As he covered her body with his, she cupped his hard cock in her hands. He let out a hard gasp as she began to stroke the tip firmly. She slid her hands down the shaft and back up again until his breathing became labored.

"In me...now!" Her voice was a forceful whisper.

Tomas parted her legs and slid a finger deeply inside her core. He moved it in and out with just enough pressure until she cried out. Resting between her thighs, he replaced his finger with his cock. The sensation of him slowly sliding into her wet heat made goosepimples rise on her skin and her cocoa nipples were tight diamonds poking his chest. She grasped his firm ass with her hands, rocking her hips.

He spoke softly in her ear and she shuddered from his warm breath. "You want me to ride you, Nahla. I want to so badly but I'm thinking of the baby. This has to be gentle."

He was as good as his word. She never imagined tender sex could be sweet torture, but it was, and she loved every agonizing moment of Tomas' brand of loving. He didn't pound her, instead thrusting firmly but carefully. She kissed his ear as he moved, rocking her hips in time with his.

Lost in pure sensation, she abandoned all thoughts beyond the moment and lifted one smooth leg to rest on his back. He went in deeper and she drew in a loud, shaky breath. She absently played with the hair at his nape and murmured her pleasure in his ear. Their coming together was easily one of the most sensual experiences of her life

He parted her lips with his tongue, keeping the rhythm as their bodies moved together toward orgasm. When it finally came for her, she gasped loudly and dug her fingernails in his back. Her core clenching around him sent him over the edge and he came, spilling himself inside of her with a pleasured groan.

Tomas raised up a bit on his forearms to look down at her. "Nahla...you are——"

Nahla placed a finger on his lips. "Shhh. You don't have to say a word. What we have is brand new and so delicate. Let's not ruin it with words." She smiled slightly.

Later, she lay in his embrace in the now dark room. Tomas wasn't a cover hog and she settled in comfortably under the blankets and sheets. She had been playing with an idea for the past hour but wasn't sure if she could pull it off without waking him. There was also her beacon becoming stronger for Sebastian, which was definitely a possibility with using powerful spells. She understood the risks but decided in a few moments time that helping Tomas would be worth it.

Nahla untangled her arms and placed her hands on his temples. He didn't stir and she breathed a sigh. *So far, so good...* She chanted ancient magick words in a whisper, laying the groundwork for her spell. Soon, a humming vibration began to spread from her hands all through her body. She spoke next to his ear, guiding his thoughts right where she needed them to be.

"Remember your father, Tomas. Remember the day you lost your magic."

Nahla sat up abruptly as a flash of light cut through the darkness of the room. Ghostly images flickered before becoming static. She had done this spell many times but never had the images appeared so solid. She was looking at a memory from Tomas's troubled past, a fight with his father.

She focused first on a much younger Tomas, probably fifteen or sixteen. His dark hair was long, falling over his shoulders and his face was more rounded. She recognized the stony expression, though. Her attention moved to his father. He was a giant of a man with the same dark hair and eyes, towering over Tomas with a look of rage.

"On judgement day, you and your mother will be condemned for using the dark arts."

Tomas didn't back down, his jaw tense as he ground out the words. "There's nothing dark about our magick, Dad. You didn't always think that. You stopped using your power out of fear you can't control it. It doesn't have to be that way."

"I stopped using the devil's power when God spoke to me in a dream," he roared.

"That's more of your ridiculous theories," Tomas fired back.

His father viciously back-handed him and he stumbled. The images began to flicker again as now grown Tomas wrestled in his sleep. Nahla took her eyes off the scene playing out in front of her to focus on him and her heart dropped. He was awake and sitting up. Suddenly, his gaze shifted beyond her to the scene in the middle of the room. His father was coming at the younger him menacingly with an extension cord dangling from one hand.

"Make it stop, Nahla." Tomas' voice was ice cold. "What you've done here, make it stop."

With a short chant, the images flickered out and disappeared, leaving the two of them in the dark room. As he moved to get up, she scrambled to stop him by grabbing his arm. He shook her off firmly and left the bed. He gathered his clothing and began dressing. His words felt like cold water dousing her.

"You just couldn't leave it the hell alone, could you? I trusted you."

Nahla reached over and flicked on the lamp. His eyes were distant, shredding her heart into tiny pieces. She wrapped the blanket around her. "I didn't mean to break your trust. I'm trying to help you regain your gift, Tomas. Your magick is a breathing, vital part of you that's just hidden under layers of pain."

His jaw clenched. "What kind of a gift lands you in the emergency room for six hours? My father beat me within an inch of my life that day."

"Your father was a madman. He clearly wanted you to

deny the magick in your ancestral line. That can only cripple you. Why are you letting him win by not trying to restore your power?"

Tomas flung on his heavy coat and reached for the door handle. He didn't look back at her. "I don't want to talk about this ever again. Understood?" At her murmured assent, he nodded. "I'll be here to pick you up for work at 10 a.m."

The door closed behind him and she closed her teary eyes. Her heart was hurting but there was also an undercurrent of anger at his stubbornness. She punched a pillow in frustration. This was not how she wanted their night to end. If Tomas Castillo thought this crusade to save him from himself was over, he was wrong by a long shot.

Gurgling. Nahla frowned, trying to identify where the sound was coming from. Her gaze lit on the pitcher of iced water on the small table and she approached it slowly, noting the steam rising from the boiling water. She blinked a few times in astonishment and a pleased smile curved her lips. Tomas, in his anger, had unwittingly done something amazing. "So much for your power being gone..." she whispered.

Thousands of miles away, Sebastian smiled in the darkness as he stretched out on his bed. Just a few moments before, he had been successful in locating Nahla's power beacon. She had used her magick and, for the first time in a long while, he was able to track her general location. She was far away but not too far for him to find her and their child. He reached for his cell phone on the nightstand. Her beacon wouldn't last for more than a day or two, so he had to be quick. Soon, he would bring her back where she belonged.

His associate picked up on the first ring. "Dante, I'm calling in a favor."

Dante's voice on the other end was smooth and calm, but Sebastian could almost hear the wheels turning in his head. "Sebastian, for all of your…assistance with our vampire faction, I imagine I owe you plenty. What can I do?"

"I've located my missing pregnant bride. I need you to plant yourself in her new world and keep a close eye on her until I'm able to get there."

"You want me to befriend her, no? Gain her trust."

"Yes, that's exactly the plan." He didn't entirely trust the vampire, but he was admittedly efficient.

"Give me the details and consider me at your service." He paused. "As long as I can continue to rely on your help."

Sebastian blew out a breath. "You, of course, have my word. My resources are still at your disposal."

———

Tomas curved the knife, cutting deeply into the pumpkin. As he finished the eyes of the jack-o-lantern, his gaze moved over to Nahla doing her carving at the next table. A few days had passed since the night spent in her room at the inn and things were still strained between them. If he was distantly polite, she was even more so. Her lingering glances in his direction told a different story.

They had signed up for decorating the town square for the Halloween Festival in a few days time. The large space was filled with dozens of darkly colorful booths, set up to offer candy and small gifts to the children. He glanced down the way to find Lisbeth and Mina waving excitedly at him and he waved back. He refused to stay in a down mood and attempted to put his situation with Nahla out of his mind.

He had been enviously watching her for the better part of

an hour. She snapped her fingers and fire burned from her fingertips to light the jack-o-lanterns with seemingly little effort. He wished he could call on his magick as easily as she could. *What if she's right about me...* The thought that he was in a prison of his own making intrigued him.

Tomas focused his energy on his hand, chanting under his breath. The magick didn't flow like it had years ago and he could feel the mental block. He sighed deeply in disappointment and tried several more times. It was no good. He was as useless as a dead battery. He looked up to find Nahla's eyes on him. She nodded with a small smile. He found himself smiling back at her, his heart catching as she approached him.

"It looks like you're trying to use your magick. Am I right?" She came to stand right in front of him. She frowned. "Or have I misread things?"

He nodded. "No, you're right. What you said the other night got me thinking that maybe I'm the whole reason why my energy won't work. Something inside my head is creating a block. Either way, I gave it my best shot and...nothing." He shrugged.

"Maybe the trouble isn't in your head, but in your heart. Painful emotions are known to suppress a witch's power. The trick is to keep trying. Don't give up, Tomas. I can help you if you let me."

His heart softened in an instant as she stood in front of him, offering her help though he knew he'd overreacted the other night. He knew he'd hurt her and all he wanted to do was make things right. He took her hand, speaking gently.

"I'm sorry about the way I spoke to you that night in your room. I don't want to leave things the way they've been between us. I, uh, would like to keep trying to fix myself, with your help."

Nahla's bright smile tugged at him. He realized how much he missed seeing it. She laced her fingers with his. "Let's make some magick together, Tomas. Literally."

———

Tomas clenched his fists as another shot of pain arced through his body. He had gone to bed a few hours earlier, exhausted from his busy day, thinking he would drift off right away. Instead, after a few minutes in bed, the wrenching pain had begun in his legs and crept its way up to his arms and chest.

He turned over onto his back, hoping for relief from the aches that felt like he was being electrocuted within. He clenched his fists again and grunted. Was this what arthritis felt like? He rubbed his shoulders and moved down his arms. As he moved his palms together, a bright light shot from them, illuminating the dark room. "What the hell…"

Tomas clapped his hands together and blue electric sparks shot out to light the room again. He noted the pain was slowly receding and sighed in relief. He hadn't experienced anything like this since he was a young teen, slowly coming into his power. What if…? He smiled as an idea came to him in his confusion and he dared to hope his magick was returning. What could've triggered it, he wondered.

He reached for his cell phone on the nightstand, then paused. He wanted Nahla to know about this possible miracle but thought it better to wait until he picked her up in the morning. As comfortable as she was with her own magick, he was certain she would know what was happening to him and how to help. He rolled over and pulled the blankets up, wearing a grin.

"You made sparks with your hands?"

Tomas nodded in response to Nahla. They both sat on the end of her bed at the inn, close enough to embrace. She wanted to fling her arms around him at the news but stopped herself. He wasn't smiling with joy at the idea of his powers returning. In fact, his brow was furrowed.

"The pain had me clenched up all over. The only thing that seemed to make it go away was shooting those sparks out of my hands." He paused, staring off for a moment. His tone was soft. "It reminds me of what I endured when I first came into my power as a teen."

Nahla's eyes welled with tears at the abuse she was sure he was recalling. She turned her head, dashing them away with a quick hand. She reminded herself he needed her strength, not a pity party. Clearing her throat. she grabbed both of his hands in hers. "Tomas, you'll just have to trust me on this. I think this was more than just a misfire of your lost power. There's a purpose for this from the spirits we call upon. I think there's a strong possibility your magick is returning." The guilt of not telling him about the boiling water pitcher weighed heavy in her gut, but she resolved to keep that to herself until she could confirm exactly what they were dealing with. She didn't want to get his hopes up too high.

Tomas rubbed a hand across his face. "But the severe body aches this time were infinitely worse than anything I ever experienced as a kid."

"Maybe it's a case of the greater the power, the greater the pain." She sighed deeply, stroking the back of his hand on her knee. "It sounds as if your magick is rogue and intermittent right now. Today, we'll work on helping you harness it and bend it to your will."

Nahla raised both of his hands in front of her face. "Do exactly what you did last night."

He clapped his hands together. Nothing. At her nod, he repeated the motion. Again, not a single spark. "It was just a misfire, obviously. I have absolutely zero chance of controlling it."

She was hesitant with her suggestion. "Try focusing on something deeply emotional to you. That sounds like a possible trigger."

His voice was flat. "You want me to think about my dad again, don't you?"

She shrugged, biting her lip. "Yes, that may work. Or think of the anguish of your last love affair."

His gaze was no longer focused on his hands. He tracked the movement of her tongue running across her bottom lip and she noted the hungry look on his face. "I'd rather think about my current love affair with you." He leaned in suddenly and placed his lips on hers.

Nahla moaned softly at his tongue playing with hers. Just as he moved to deepen the kiss, a series of sparks arced between their joined lips. "Ouch! You just shocked me." She jerked back, covering her mouth and smiling at his amazed expression. "But, you did it again like you did last night."

She clapped her hands in front of her, whispering an ancient chant. A ball of fire appeared between her palms. "Try again, Tomas. You can do this. Focus your energy on your raw emotions."

He again clapped his hands together and, on his third try, sparks flew wildly for long moments. He spoke the chant loudly and his eyes widened as they became a ball of pure electricity. "Holy shit, it worked!"

"Do you feel a shift in the mental block in your mind?"

"A little, but not much." The ball of sparks between his hands disappeared and he dropped them in his lap. "I was thinking about my dad, a woman who broke my heart, and finally you. So, I'm guessing I need to be either pissed off or turned on sexually to make my magick work," He grunted in frustration.

Nahla snuffed out on her fireball and placed her hands on his face. "I suspect this is only the beginning. As we work more together, you may eventually be able to control it again." She looked deeply into his eyes. "I didn't want you to have unrealistic expectations, so I kept it from you. The other night here in my room, when you were furious with me, you transferred that anger to a pitcher of water on the table. Tomas...you boiled it."

"I did what?"

A small smile curved her full lips. "Your magick did it. It must've been you. That's more proof that your magick isn't gone, it's just buried beneath that mental block that protected you for so many years."

He whispered in Spanish under his breath and looked over at the fresh pitcher of ice water. "Should I intentionally try it again?"

Nahla shook her head. "I don't think so. Remember, baby steps." Right on cue, her baby began tap dancing in her belly and her laughter tinkled. "Speaking of which, it's probably time for me to eat. How about we sit down for dinner in the Cat's Paw downstairs?"

Tomas grinned. "I'm happy to join you."

Nahla sat at the table she and Tomas had picked out,

staring through the glass as the vibrant fingers of sunlight stretched across the floor. Dusk was swiftly on its way and she was able to see a star or two. Tomas had excused himself a few moments before to take an important phone call.

She spotted the man across the room, staring at her just as their server placed the glasses of iced tea on the table. Smiling in thanks as she moved away, Nahla sipped her tea and curiously returned her gaze to the handsome, dark haired man. Still staring. She hastily broke off eye contact as he left his table to saunter over to hers.

As he approached, her senses flew off the charts. He smiled as he stood across the table. "Vampire," she murmured aloud.

The vamp nodded and gestured at the empty chair. "May I?" He sat down, his eyes scanning her face.

"Sure. You should know that I'm dining with someone. He'll be back any minute."

His lips tilted upwards. "I'm a vampire, yes. And you come from a fae clan." He inclined his head. "Many vampires are just as sensitive to vibrations as you are. My gut instincts tell me you're a fae witch with great power. Also, you smell delicious. All the fae do."

He chuckled at her raised eyebrow. "Should I be worried about you lusting after my blood?"

"No, not one bit. My diet is restricted to animal blood only. Forgive my intrusion. I'm Nikolai Murik and I'm just passing through. I haven't encountered a witch with such power in many years. I, of course, had to meet you."

Nahla nodded. "Are you traveling for business? If so, how on earth did you end up here in Catnip?"

He pinned her with his intense gaze again. "Yes. A good

friend told me I shouldn't miss this charming little town. I'm only here until the end of the Halloween Festival."

She spotted Tomas making his way across the diner and Nikolai stood up abruptly. "It was a pleasure to meet you…?"

"My name is Nahla." She shook his outstretched hand.

"Enjoy your evening." He brushed past Tomas, heading toward the lobby of the inn.

Tomas sat down wearing a bemused expression. "Who was that? And, did you catch he's a vamp?"

Nahla sipped her tea. "Yes. So, you picked up on his vibration, too?

"Yes, with the little bit of power I have left. We don't see too many of those around here. Burlington and the other major cities are filled with them. What did he want?"

Nahla gave him a teasing glance. "He was impressed with the way my blood smells. Relax, Tomas. He seems pretty harmless." She slid a menu across the table to him. "I'm starving. Let's get the food ordered."

He grunted. "Given your situation with Caldecott, I don't trust anyone you don't know trying to get close to you."

She shrugged. "He seemed like a nice enough guy. He backed off politely once I told him I had already had a dinner date." She clutched his hand. "You worry about me more than I worry about me. Knowing Sebastian, if he knew where I was, he would have already showed up here. I feel safe here, Tomas. I feel safe…with you." She smiled gently.

"I promised to protect you, Nahla. I won't fail you on that."

They enjoyed a savory meal before heading outdoors to walk the grounds of the inn. The moon peeked out from among the tall trees, bathing both of them in its glow. Nahla and Tomas slowed to a stop under the canopy of stars. He caught her delicate hand in his and planted a kiss on her fingertips.

"I'm enchanted with you, runaway witch," he murmured, kissing the corner of her lips. "Have you given any thought to my offer and staying here in Catnip with me until after the baby is born? It'll give you time to get back on your feet."

She caught his lips with hers before speaking. "I'm tempted like you wouldn't believe, but I don't want to bring trouble to your door. Let me think it over. Sebastian isn't your problem."

"He's my problem now." He heaved a deep sigh. "I have an early morning tomorrow at the hospital in Burlington. I'll pick you up and take you to my home an hour earlier, if that's good with you."

She nodded. "That works out perfectly. I still have more sorting and such to do in your office."

"I'll walk you to your room, then."

It was harder than she ever thought possible to wish him good night at her door. She wanted him to join her in her bed tonight, but she stopped to consider the consequences. Making love with him again would only cement her attachment to him. Tomas was a gentleman and a good man. He didn't deserve to be burdened with her problems.

After she chastely kissed him, he stood back. Desire smoldered in his eyes. Good lord, he looked like he wanted to taste her everywhere. Instead, he nodded and headed down the hallway.

"Good night, Nahla." The laughter was evident in his tone and she scowled at his retreating back. Damn him – he knew all about her struggles to distance herself from him romantically. She closed the door and leaned back against it eyes closed for a moment. *How much longer before we give in to each other?*

Sebastian listened to Dante's account of Nahla's dinner that evening with the warlock in Catnip, especially focused on the kiss they had shared. He was more than annoyed, snapping the pen he held in half. "Tell me what you know about this Tomas Castillo."

The vampire on the other end relayed what he had uncovered about the other warlock and Sebastian seethed in silence. Long moments passed before he clipped out each word. "Stay on her, but from a safe distance. I'm flying out to meet you tomorrow."

"And have you discovered my queen's resting place?"

"I have made headway on that. We'll discuss this tomorrow."

Sebastian abruptly ended the call and leaned back in his black leather chair, contemplating his next move. Catherine called out to him, disrupting his dark thoughts. "I'm coming to bed now, sweetheart."

Damn. He'd wanted to quickly use his magick to check for Nahla's beacon, but there was no time to tonight. He felt confident that, as long as she was in that town with the other warlock, Tomas Castillo, she wouldn't go anywhere else. He flipped off the lamp and left his study.

The next morning, Nahla sat in the plush chair in Tomas' office. She had spent the last two hours mostly lost in thought, managing to get a decent amount of work done.

"Knock, knock." There was a sharp rap on the door and Lisbeth poked her head in. "I don't want to interrupt what you're doing for too long. Mina's camped out on the living room sofa, watching cartoons, so I thought now would be a good time to talk for a bit."

Nahla smiled gently, waving her in. "To be honest, I've spent most of the morning daydreaming my way out of this situation with Sebastian."

Lisbeth snorted. "If only daydreams were dollar bills."

Nahla nodded. "Exactly my thoughts, too." She sighed heavily. "I don't want to burden Tomas any more than I have to."

The other witch's mouth gaped open for a moment. "Burden? You honestly think you're a burden to him? No. no. Nahla, from what I've seen and heard, Tomas is doing all of this because...well..."

"Because...?" Nahla prompted, her mouth suddenly going dry.

Lisbeth shrugged. "It's really none of my business, but I think he's in love with you." She held her hands up. "Just my best guess."

Nahla went silent for several moments. "Lisbeth, do you know about his...problem?"

"You mean his lost magick? Sure. We had a brief conversation about it when Mina and I first came here."

"Well, I've been helping him restore it. I think maybe he needs my help as much as I need his. We're just two friends helping each other until it's time to part ways. We both have lives to get back to."

Lisbeth's expression spoke volumes with a raised eyebrow. "I honestly think he wants to be a more permanent part of your life." She patted Nahla's hand. "Please just consider the idea that he loves you and what that could mean for you." She headed for the door and stood there for a long moment. "He's a truly good man and you both deserve the best. Which, I think, is each other." With a smile, she was gone, closing the door behind her.

Nahala drew in shaky breaths as she considered Lisbeth's words. She licked her dry lips, while her mind grappled with the idea that Tomas' feelings went deeper than taking care of her as his ward. Erotic images of them together in her bed at the inn tumbled around her mind. Maybe he didn't just need her help with his magick...?

The baby poked her with sturdy limbs, and she went right back to thinking about Sebastian. For the moment, she resolved to stay focused on her nightmare situation. She would decide what do with Tomas once this was over. Her mind gave her one last scorching memory of Tomas' hips moving between her spread thighs. Her panties dampened and her core throbbed with need.

She hastily reached for her water bottle and drank deeply.

SEVEN

"Thank you for doing this with me." Nahla gestured at the ultrasound unit. Tomas had brought her into the clinic in town where he worked during the week. She was lying on the bed, dressed in a hospital gown and draped with a thin white sheet. "It's time to check up on my little guy."

Tomas' eyebrows lifted. "You know it's a boy?"

She nodded. "Yes, I've known for a few months. Sebastian was with me for the first ultrasound and he kept going on and on about what a powerful warlock the baby will be. I guess he has no use for a baby girl. Either way, this is my child, not his."

The ultrasound technician rapped on the door and entered. She greeted them and exchanged pleasantries with Tomas. He took a seat in the corner as she prepared Nahla for the ultrasound. She squirmed at the cold gel on her exposed belly before reaching out a hand to Tomas.

"I'd like you to be a part of this. If you don't mind, of course."

Tomas smiled at her and moved his chair next to her. He took her hand in his. "Of course."

The technician moved the wand across her belly slowly and, bit by bit, her baby was revealed. Nahla's heart thumped with overwhelming love and excitement as her son scrunched up his little face and moved around. She felt a firm kick and let out a small laugh. "He's so much bigger now."

Her gaze traveled from the screen to Tomas. His voice was soft with wonder. "He's beautiful, Nahla. Perfect in every way."

Later, they stood at the clinic's front desk as she signed necessary paperwork. He cleared his throat. "So, do you plan to stay here with me until after the baby's born? As I told you before, I can quietly arrange for your care."

"Yes, I'm taking you up on your offer. All I need is a few weeks after he's born to make permanent living arrangements back in Los Angeles. My mom will be a great help. With all the evidence you and the Underground have given me about Sebastian, I don't think freeing myself from him legally will be a problem."

Tomas' brows came together. Was that a shadow of disappointment in his eyes? "Yes, of course you're going back to L.A.," he murmured. "Your life is there."

There was a part of her that wanted him to give her a reason to stay with him as his lover. Another part of her reasoned that they were destined to simply help each other as friends and that was the end of it. They sizzled together, in bed and out, but off- the -charts chemistry wasn't always a sign of happily ever after.

On the drive back, Nahla kept her eyes on the scene flying by outside the car window. She couldn't even look at him without it breaking her heart a little and the last thing she wanted was to engage in meaningless small talk with him when there were so many words between them left unspoken.

He pulled the car in front of the Autumn Moon Inn and killed the engine. She decided in an instant that she wasn't ready to let him go home. Pasting a cheerful smile on her face, she turned to him. "We can start the groundwork for restoring your magick right now, if you want to."

Tomas drew in a deep breath and exhaled, his hands gripping the steering wheel. "Sure. Why not? I guess it's worth a shot."

They made their way through the lobby and upstairs to her room. Once he stepped inside, flashbacks of their passionate night together assailed her. She found it hard not to remember the lean muscles and perfect abs as he shrugged off his coat.

Nahla moved across the room, clearing her throat nervously before she spoke. She lifted a small midnight blue case and set it on the bed. "This is one of my bags of tricks." He came to stand next to her as she pulled out a few candles and a small bag of pungent herbs. "Both of these will aid your concentration."

Once she completed the setup with some of the candles lit and the herbs sprinkled, she gestured for him to join her on the bed. He dutifully sat and she gripped his hands tightly. "Tomas, close your eyes and relax."

He rolled his shoulders and did as she instructed. "Ok, what's next?

"I think that your mental block's trigger is intense emotional pain. Whenever you recall that distress with your father, your mind moves in to protect you. We're going to try to move that block just a little. Focus your thoughts and energy on your feelings that day he hurt you. Don't skip ahead on the traumatic parts. Play out the scene from beginning to end."

When he tensed, she knew she was on the right path to helping him. "I tried to forget that day for a reason."

Nahla held his hands tighter. "I know. But now you need to recall it with crystal clarity."

"Oh God...the pain of that cord coming down on my back. I see my mom grabbing his arm and he turned on her."

She put one unlit candle in his hand. "You're doing fine," she said softly. "Now, remember how you felt right then and hold on to that. Next, focus your whole energy on the candle in your hand and light the wick. You can do it."

He trembled with the effort and began to chant. She joined him in speaking the ancient words and, after long moments of nothing, a tiny flame sprang upwards from the candle's wick. Her eyes widened in surprise and she excitedly tapped his shoulder.

"Tomas, look!"

He cracked one eye open and swore under his breath in Spanish with a grin. "After years of nothing..."

"You just needed someone to help you through this. Two witches' energies combined are always better than one." Nahla was warm and tingly all over at the expression of joy on his face.

She cleared her throat meaningfully. "Now, this may be a bit more challenging. What's your superpower?"

He stared at her blankly. "My what?"

She smiled gently. "You know, your special power as a warlock. Every one of us is imprinted with one by the spirits when we're born, right? Mine is wrangling the fire element."

His expression was mournful. 'When I was a young boy, back before my dad went crazy, I could bend time."

Nahla's brows shot up in surprise. "Oh, my. That's a rare gift. Let's try to reawaken that part of your magick." She drew a circle of flame in the air, skillfully adding a giant lens in the middle. Next, she took the unlit candle and grabbed up the lighter. "Try to manipulate time within the confines of this room. We'll use the burning candle as a measure."

"I doubt I have that power anymore, but I'll give it a go." He murmured the words with perfect recall. As he spoke, Nahla moved the lit candle back and forth behind the lens in the air she had created. Nothing happened for long moments and the disappointment was palpable. Tomas shivered as the confidence in his voice increased, his eyes closed tightly.

She moved the burning candle behind the lens again and gasped. Behind the lens, the candle now appeared to have melted down significantly. When she moved it away from the lens, the candle appeared brand new and unused. She didn't dare interrupt him as she noted the bedside clock had stopped ticking. He opened his eyes and smiled as she moved the candle to show him what he had done.

"Son of a bitch, I did it." He laughed. "I made time in this room go back an hour and then forward one hour." He sighed. "The problem is I'm drained. It never would've taken all my energy to do any spell before I lost my magick." He whispered a few words and the clock ticked off the seconds again.

Nahla gave him a grin, blowing out the candle. "In time, Tomas. Your power will return, I'm sure of it." She waved one hand in the air, erasing her circle lens of flame.

Tomas pulled her into a tight embrace and spoke low in her ear. "I'm in awe of you right now." He kissed her cheek softly and she moved until their lips met. She sighed as his tongue traced the pout of her bottom lip. Disappointment flooded through her when he suddenly released her. "I'd better go. With the festival starting tomorrow, I have a few last minute things to handle. You should rest, too."

Nahla nodded, keeping her expression neutral. "You're right. I also need to check in with my mom in L.A. We'll work more on this later." Her lips curved in a small smile.

He put on his coat and strode to the door. He looked back at her with a grin. "Thank you...for this. Sleep well tonight. I'll be here in the early afternoon to pick you up for the festival."

The door closed behind him and her shoulders sagged under the weight of what had just happened. All of it. She was confident that, in time, Tomas would be back in tune with his magick. She wasn't as confident that leaving him and returning to L.A. was the right thing to do. *If only he gave me a reason to stay...*

Later, after a brief phone call with her mom, Nahla settled herself into the makeshift circle on the floor of the room, created from chalk and a few candles she had brought with her. She liberally sprinkled a few herbs from her plastic bags. Curiosity had the best of her, and she had a driving need to decipher the message the spirits were sending her,

She murmured a few chants and smiled approvingly when the fire ball she had conjured in her palms ignited into a controlled blaze when she set it in the center of the circle. "Ancient Ones, explain the message you've sent to me. I call upon you for clarification."

The flames leapt higher for long moments in the silence before a vision appeared. Nahla's lips parted in surprise. She was looking into a grave and slowly the dead occupant was revealed. Feminine hands, gnarled with great age appeared, the nails still painted crimson. The woman's face was shriveled, the rest of her desiccated. Long blonde hair streamed from her dead scalp down over her breasts. Something deep and primal urged Nahla to look away and forget she had ever summoned the vision.

As she reached to blow out the candles, paralysis struck, and she had no choice but to continue watching the horrific scene unfold. The woman's face contorted into a hellish grin. "Come closer, witch." Nahla heard the words clearly in her mind, as if the woman was speaking in her ear. This was the most evil thing she had ever witnessed and she had dealt with tons of wicked spirits. She intuited, without doubt, the being was trying to draw on her power

The instinct for survival kicked in and Nahla struggled to return to the realm of the living. She feverishly chanted and pushed against the oppressive spirit. One of the guardians of the dead whispered in her ear, "What is dead, should remain dead." With a whoosh of the flames dying out, her paralysis shattered, and the vision evaporated into the ether.

Nahla sagged limply against the bottom of the bed, harsh breaths coming from her lips. Her curiosity had morphed into terror. Maybe it was better to never know what the spirits meant if she had to endure that whole scene again. It was possible she was an old witch, traveling the underworld, whose light had yet to be extinguished. Whoever the woman was, she had a dark and twisted essence. And she was definitely not dead. Not completely.

"So, is decorating the new way pregnant women stay fit?"

Nahla looked up from the orange and gold streamer she was attaching to the table. It was dusk on the day of the Halloween Festival in town, so she wasn't overly surprised by her visitor. She gave him a smile, setting aside the stapler gun. "Nikolai, right? So nice to see you. You've kept to yourself at the inn. I guessed that you would have zero interest in all this."

He shrugged, returning her smile. "And miss all the excitement in this quaint, little town? Not a chance." He gestured at her table full of colorful decorations. "You decided to volunteer tonight?"

"Just with the set-up. I won't be actually working a table or booth tonight." She patted her rounded tummy. "Any activity helps me stay fit."

Nikolai chuckled. "And, will your companion from the inn's diner also be joining you tonight?"

Nahla's smile was faint as she nodded. "You mean Tomas? Yes, he'll be here."

"It's good you're not alone here in town. Your…friend Tomas, he's obviously keeping you safe."

Nahla's back went rigid and she observed him warily. "Safe from what?"

"Oh, all the ghouls and maybe a vampire or two out here this evening. We're approaching the witching hour soon, you know."

She relaxed at his teasing tone, twining another streamer. "I'm protected in the best ways possible."

Nikolai inclined his head. "Yes, it appears you are. I'll leave you to your project. Hopefully, our paths will cross again later tonight." With a casual wave, he strode away from the table.

Tomas stood beside Nahla at one of the booths that was selling steaming apple cider. He looked her over slowly as she ordered, taking in the simple black dress and colorful Mardi Gras mask Lisbeth had scrounged up to lend to her. He wore his warlock cape. He knew she would be out of his life in a few months, but he still couldn't keep her out of thoughts.

And erotic fantasies on nights he lay awake in his cold, lonely bed. He sipped at his cider with a frown. Nahla turned to him, her own cup in her hands.

She looked around the town square for a few moments. The Halloween Festival was in full swing, with decorated booths, streamers and balloons, and jack-o-lanterns at every turn. Rubbing her belly with one hand, she smiled. "I think he's excited by all the noise." As if to emphasize her point, two children dressed in clown costumes ran by them, screaming.

"If this all gets to be too much, we can leave. Just say the word."

She sipped from her cup and shook her head. "I'm fine. I don't want to miss all this tonight. All Hallows Eve only comes once a year. What self-respecting witch would bow out before midnight?"

Tomas grunted. "I have skipped this festival a few times in the past when the fact that I had no magick to offer the world got to me."

She patted his hand. "I believe that soon you won't have to worry about your magick ever again. We made progress, right?"

He shrugged. "It could lead me back to nothing again, though. There's a difference between lighting a match and casting a spell. I could fail at that. Again."

"Progress is progress. Your power isn't gone, it's just banked. I fully believe that you'll be casting spells again in no time."

Tomas noted the strained creases on her forehead and took her hand in his. "I know you're still worried about that vision of the dead woman in the casket. Don't give it another thought."

Nahla sighed deeply. "I wish I could but she was just so… evil. I could sense it, even before she spoke to me. The spirits are in deep unrest about her."

"I'm sure she's just an old, long buried witch, making her final gasps."

"But what are the guardian spirits trying to tell us? "The dead should remain dead? What does that have to do with this particular woman?"

"Probably nothing. You and I both know what happens when the spirits decide to play around. They love to, sometimes, confound witches with their mystical messages." He raised her hand to his lips.

Lisbeth emerged from the crowd, approaching them with Mina in hand. She wore a black witch hat and colorful cape. "Hi, you two. This is all so festive and exciting."

"Boo!" Tomas made a scary face at Mina, who stood before him in a small Batman costume, complete with mask. She laughed delightedly and tugged at Nahla's hand. "Will your baby be here soon?"

She smiled down at the little girl. "Oh, absolutely."

Mina's attention was soon caught by the booth in the distance handing out balloons and she begged Lisbeth to go. With a wave, the two set off in that direction. Nahla linked her arm through Tomas' and they wandered around the square. By the second lap, she was tired so he suggested they sit down on one of the benches.

Longing to make every moment with her last as long as possible, he asked her about her life in Los Angeles. She was animated as she spoke about her family and experiences as a graduate student and Tomas felt a tug of envy that her life was so full of love and aspirations. His own was accomplished but ultimately filled with nothing other than his own loneliness. He admitted to himself that she filled that troubling void whenever they were together.

Lisbeth came running to them, waving her hands frantically. "Oh, please help me! It's Mina—she's disappeared. We were picking out balloons and I turned my back for a minute, and she was gone. Some lady saw her holding hands with a tall blond man, walking through the crowd. She's so damn friendly."

Tomas rose to his feet quickly. "Where is this lady who saw her?"

Nahla came to her feet and clutched his arm in a tight grip. Her expression was tense. "That won't do us any good now. He's found me. I'm sure it's my ex, Sebastian, who has her. He's sending a message to me."

Tomas swore loudly. 'We need to involve the Witches Council police, then. He's dangerous as hell."

Lisbeth wiped away tears. "I tried to locate her beacon, but I can't find her."

Nahla nodded, her expression grave. "He's cloaked them both. His magick is very powerful, which is why I haven't sensed him here in the area."

Tomas suddenly had an idea. He turned to her. "The vision spell you did the other night—can you do it again without Mina here?"

"I can use the bond between Lisbeth and Mina to do it. We can see her whereabouts with Sebastian and use it to track her. We'll need somewhere private and dark."

Tomas nodded, his jaw tense. "Let's move to the outer part of the town square."

Nahla gripped Tomas' and Lisbeth's hands, praying silently for a miracle. They stood in a dark, secluded area on the outskirts of the Town Square, having formed a circle. She could sense strong magick coming from the other witch and her hopes raised. The two of them would need to compensate for Tomas' lesser energy.

She looked at Lisbeth and nodded. "It's go time."

The three of them began chanting the words of an ancient spell. The dead silence punctuated their voices and Nahla shuddered, but she continued, not missing a beat. The towering trees overhead rustled as a strong wind suddenly kicked up. Fallen leaves flurried around them as a muted light drew from their joined hands.

They all looked as flickering images appeared. She immediately recognized Sebastian walking through a wooded area. Damn it—he was alone. No sign of little Mina was a glaring red flag. She willed herself not to panic and refocused on chanting. The powerful warlock came to a stop and the spell revealed the girl lying deathly still on the dirt and leaves.

Lisbeth cried out and Nahla clutched her hand tighter. "He's unstable, but not stupid. Killing a witch's child carries a heavy penalty. He could be confined for life or have his magick bound for years. He wouldn't risk that just to get to me. He probably has her in a thrall spell."

Tomas' voice was grim. "It looks like an area down by the river which I'm very familiar with. I'll call the Council police to meet us there."

They all whispered their gratitude to the spirits and broke the spell. The images died away as Lisbeth wiped her eyes. "I want this bastard to pay. Mina...she's just a baby."

They made the trek to Tomas' car parked on a side street a few blocks away and piled in. He started the car, revving the engine, before smoothly pulling out of the spot and heading down the street. Their silence was tense and spoke volumes of abject fear. No one was more fearful than Nahla. She instinctively rubbed her rounded belly, thinking of the eventual trade-off with Sebastian. She already knew his purpose—her and her child in exchange for Mina.

Her heart raced but she tamped down the fear and let her anger rise. She would sacrifice her freedom for Mina, without question. Her only option was to escape him again, at some point. For now, she would turn herself over to him, if necessary. After several minutes, the scenery changed from brightly lit streets and cottages to the wooded area of the town. Soon, she could hear the roar of rushing water.

Tomas parked the car in a clearing and killed the engine. He pulled his cell phone from his pocket. "The Council police are several miles away but—"

A bright light exploded in the distance and dread tugged at Nahla. "It's Sebastian's signal, no doubt. He knows I'm here and wants me to come to him."

"Oh, my baby," Lisbeth murmured.

"This whole thing has gone far enough. You wouldn't be in this situation if it weren't for me. I'm going to try to take him down and subdue him for the Council cops to handle." Nahla was out of the front seat like a shot and making her way through the woods. She heard Tomas and Lisbeth shouting to her, but she kept going.

She had never been by the river and it was dark, except for the moonlight and Sebastian's signal. Trudging on, she welcomed the night sounds of the animals echoing. "What am I doing?" she muttered. She had acted impulsively and now knew she needed Tomas and Lisbeth for backup. She turned around to head back the way she came. Directly behind her, Nikolai stood. The slash of moonlight illuminated his face and he wore the strangest smile.

"No," he said softly. "It's a bit late to turn around now, little Nahla."

She frowned. "What are you talking..." Her eyes widened. "Oh, God, you're in on this thing with Sebastian, aren't you?"

He grabbed her arms and turned her back around. He moved them forward through the brush, his words right by her ear. "If it's any consolation, I also think Sebastian will be a terrible father."

Eventually, they came to another clearing in the woods and stopped short. Sebastian was perched on a large rock, wearing a smug smile. He waved a hand, igniting a bushel of branches. Mina lie motionless at his feet. He opened his arms wide.

"There you are, Nahla. I was becoming very annoyed with you hiding from me. Surely you didn't think I was just going to give up."

"God, yes, I wanted to be free from you, so I hid. Any sane witch would." Her lip lifted. "That says a lot about your wife. You know, the one you've had for ten years."

His smile slipped and his brows thundered together. "You've been talking to the wrong people."

"But you didn't deny it." She blew out a deep breath, pretending to be resigned to her fate. "The Council police are on their way. Awaken Mina from the thrall you have her under and I'll go with you. We can be long gone by the time they get here."

She murmured a chant under her breath, sending her magick out to him. He immediately raised a hand, redirecting her energy upwards. A heavy tree branch sparked and crashed down behind him. He chuckled darkly.

"That was amusing but stupid. If you don't play by my

rules, the child will stay in my sleep thrall for months. Maybe even years, if I decide it." He extended a hand. "Come back to me, Nahla. I've been lost without you. Is life with me really so unbearable?"

"I'm not your wife. You already have one." She clipped every word.

Sebastian's smile was unpleasant. "We'll discuss that later. I want you and my child back with me. Now."

Nahla, fearful for Mina, took a tentative step forward. A strong hand clamped down on her arm and she whipped around. Tomas and Lisbeth had her flanked on either side. He shook his head slowly.

"You should've stayed with us at the car." He moved in front of her and turned his attention to the warlock. "You have no business here. The Council police are coming for you. Give us Mina and disappear. You may remain a free man. It's our word against yours."

Sebastian's laughter grated. "I don't sense very much power coming from you. What kind of a warlock are you?"

"One that will take you down, you bastard."

Nahla's stomach dropped as the warlock inclined his head. He had taken it as a direct challenge. He wouldn't back down, but neither would Tomas. Her fledgling Tomas.

"If you want the child, then come and get her."

Tomas whispered a prayer and closed his eyes. He reached out his hands to Nahla and Lisbeth. They formed a circle as he heaved a deep breath. His failure to help could mean a lifetime of sleep with Mina in her thrall. "Power of three," he said softly.

A whirlwind blaze ignited within their circle as they spoke ancient words and lifted above them. A tugging began deep in his gut and he felt the mental block move just a bit. The pillar of fire leapt at Sebastian, consuming him for a few moments. He raised his hands and sent it tumbling to the riverbank.

His blood roared in his ears at the adrenaline rush and he had trouble making out Nahla's words. "Go back to that day with your father in your mind. Remember the pain and your magick slipping away from you. Hold on to it!"

Tomas did as she said, focusing his energy on Sebastian. The memory came, bitter and palpable, and he held on to it like a drowning man. The block in his mind moved just a little more and he felt a small burst of power. He chanted a familiar litany, willing the other warlock's throat to close.

Across the distance, Sebastian began choking, clutching his throat for long moments. He raised one hand, directing the energy back at Tomas. He suddenly couldn't breathe. Trying to gulp down air put a strain on his heart and the beating pounded his ears. Still, Nahla and Lisbeth held his hands tightly.

"Fight it with everything in you, Tomas."

Nahla's words helped him center himself. He gasped, fighting to remain conscious. He let the memory come back in a rush. He was lost in the moment in time. His father yelling in his face, his mother pushed backwards with an angry hand, the cord coming down on his back over and over. Using a burst of power, he blocked Sebastian's energy, sucking down gulps of air.

The other warlock narrowed his eyes and took a few steps toward Nahla. He tapped his wristwatch. "Enough of this. I'm losing precious escape time. Nahla, come to me or I'll destroy him. You know I can."

Tomas heard her tormented groan and grabbed her arm as she moved toward Sebastian. "No! This is our fight together, remember?" The silver moonlight illuminated the tears running down her cheeks and rage consumed him. He focused his attention on the other warlock, clapping his hands together. A sphere of electricity lit up and he threw it into the open space between them, creating a barrier surrounding the other warlock.

Sebastian rushed toward them and bounced backwards. He grunted, reaching out a hand to touch the wall of electric currents and snatched it back at the crackling sound. His face twisted into a scowl. "Nahla, end this now. It's only a matter of time before I break through this and make your little friend pay."

Fear snaked up Tomas' spine as the energy shifted within him. He was exhausted and his wall wouldn't hold for much longer. "Give us Mina and I'll let you out."

Sebastian smirked. "You know the terms. Nahla in exchange for the little girl." He spun his hands in the air as he chanted words of the darkest magick. Tomas yelped in pain as his box of electricity was turned against him and he was now trapped within it. He heard Nahla scream as he weakly dropped to his knees.

The other warlock quickly grabbed Nahla's arms and held her firmly against him. He spoke harshly to a terrified Lisbeth. "I'll release my thrall on your child once Nahla and I are far from here. A deal is a deal, I guess." He gestured at Tomas. "He's going to die in there."

Tomas groaned in agony as his energy ebbed and flowed within him. His magick was out of control. He tried to stand up, powerless to stop Sebastian as he moved Nahla away from the clearing, headed for the deep woods. He knew he wasn't far from losing consciousness as she screamed his name again and again.

Fear was swiftly replaced with pure adrenaline rage. It was

a kaleidoscope of images, both from the past and present. *The cord on my back…my mom fighting back….Nahla shouting.* His eyes flickered open and he saw a struggling Nahla with Sebastian at the edge of the clearing. His energy shifted and he came to his feet. The dam broke in his mind and…he was free. He chanted and waved his hand.

The whispering wind came to a standstill, as did all the nocturnal wood creatures. The fire no longer crackled and danced. Tomas smiled wearily at Lisbeth as his cage disappeared. "What have you done?" she whispered.

"I stopped time here in this part of the woods." He gestured at Sebastian and the vampire watching from the sidelines, both frozen in mid motion. He watched as Nahla back-peddled cautiously from the other warlock. She turned and ran towards Tomas. He swept her into his arms, kissing her forehead.

"Let me take care of this while I still can. I'm so tired and I don't know how long my magick can hold on." He slowly approached Sebastian, creating a sphere of electricity and manipulating into a lasso. He quickly bound the warlock's arms with his energy and roughly shoved him to a sitting position on the dirt. With a few murmured words, time resumed in the clearing. The gentle wind brushed his face and he sucked it in deeply.

Lisbeth rushed from his side to cradle her daughter in her arms. Nahla's gentle hands rubbed his back as he trembled. He looked at her.

"You did it, Tomas. You saved the day." Her warm smile flooded through him.

He gave her a crooked smile as his heart rate slowly returned to normal. "My power came back in a rush, but I think I couldn't have done it without our power of three." He stroked her cheek. "Sebastian is a monster, Nahla. I don't understand how—"

She placed one finger to his lips. "I can't believe I was so naïve, either."

They turned their attention to a slowly awakening Mina. "Mommy?"

Lisbeth gave them a bright smile, wiping away tears. "Thank you both." She looked down at her daughter, speaking soft words of comfort.

Nahla kicked Sebastian's limp body. "Good thing you bound this bastard. He's not dead, which is a shame, but he is out cold. Now's the perfect time to temporarily restrict his movement and his power."

As they finished a binding spell, a team of uniformed men burst into the clearing, followed by a tall woman. A startled Nahla clung to him and he kissed her forehead. "It's ok. Finally, the reinforcements are here."

He looked over to the other side of the clearing and zeroed in on Nikolai still hiding in the brush. Their eyes met and he smiled darkly, giving them a two-finger salute. "Long live the vampire queen. Long live Galina Saburova," he said sharply. The woods soon swallowed him in the shadows.

The officer leading the crew barked orders as he approached them. The crew quickly surrounded Sebastian, handcuffing him. "Hey, Tomas. Thanks for the phone call. We've been tracking Sebastian Caldecott for weeks." He turned his gaze to Nahla. "I'm Officer Spencer from the Witches' Council Police Agency. You must be Nahla Gregory."

"Yes, I am. But...why have you been tracking Sebastian?"

"Unfortunately, you're not his only stalking victim. He did this to another young witch up in Seattle. She barely escaped with her sanity after the nightmare he had her in. He's also wanted for his connections to a dangerous vampire faction."

The other officers raised a dazed Sebastian to his feet. The woman stopped them from escorting him away. Tomas couldn't make out the conversation, but her hand cracked sharply across the warlock's face. As the team led him away, she approached them.

The tall woman removed her hood, revealing long dark blonde hair, high cheekbones, and a slash of crimson lips. She spoke smoothly. "Ms. Gregory. I'm Catherine Caldecott, Sebastian's wife. I wish we had met under better circumstances." She gestured at Nahla's belly. 'I take it the child is his?'"

Nahla nodded. "Hello, Mrs. Caldecott. Yes, my baby is his, though I wish I could say otherwise."

Catherine waved a hand. "You and your child are safe from my husband. I promise you, once the courts are finished with him, he won't be anyone's problem ever again." Her lips lifted in a grim smile. "Not even mine. Should the unfortunate day ever come when he is freed, keep your child as far away from Sebastian Caldecott as you can. I wish you all well."

She turned and left the clearing, following behind the team. Officer Spencer assured Nahla that she was safe to return home. Tomas' disappointment was sharp. There was no reason for her to stay in Catnip. No reason at all. Even though he knew he loved her, maybe it wouldn't be enough to make her stay. *Unless...*

EIGHT

After Tomas made certain that Lisbeth and Mina were settled in at his home, he drove Nahla back to the Autumn Moon Inn. The ride back was quiet, with minimal conversation between them. She had a lot to process. Free. She was forever free of Sebastian and could return home tomorrow, if she wanted to. Her old life was calling to her, but she pondered her attachment to Tomas and the life she had started to make in Catnip.

Nahla leaned on him as he turned the key in the lock to her room. He helped her inside and closed the door behind them. She turned on the lamp on the nightstand. Facing him, she was caught by the tenderness she saw in his eyes. "Thank you," she whispered.

He had her in his embrace before she could say another word. "No, thank you. These past few weeks with you have been the best time of my life. You forced me to face my demons and helped me restore my magick, which I thought was gone for good." He brushed her lips with his. 'I guess you'll be heading home soon."

A knot of longing formed in her belly. He expected her to leave. *What other ending can there be...?* She had other ideas of saying goodbyes. Throwing caution away, she kissed him. Her little tongue darted around his lips, separating them. His passionate response was all she needed to spur her on.

Nahla took the lead, helping him undress. She savored every stroke and caress of his naked body. He made short work of removing her dress, bra and panties. Their clothes were a pile on the floor when he carried her to the bed. His fingertips first traced every curve before his firm hands cupped her breasts.

His mouth at her nipples had her gasping in pleasure. His fingertips stroking her warm, wet core made her call out his name. She returned the favor by grasping his hard cock in her hands. Laying him back on the bed, she used her tongue in inventive ways all over his body until she again reached his cock. She encircled the tip with her mouth, sucking softly. Looking up, she noted with satisfaction how his eyes were tightly closed and how his hands gripped the bed covers. She wanted to bring him over.

Before she could continue the torment, he reversed their positions. He smiled at her, then caressed her body as he lowered himself between her spread thighs. His tongue gently traced her core, moving up to flick her sensitive bud. She cried out, gripping his hair in both hands. When he decided she'd had enough, he moved up and entered her with one smooth stroke.

Their coming together was bittersweet this time. No less passionate than the first time, but with a note of sadness. He hadn't asked her to stay and that was that. Pleasure came over her in waves and when she found her release, she moved her hips in time with his until he came, whispering her name over and over.

Nahla lay wrapped in Tomas' embrace, feeling secure for the first time in months. Her words were a soft murmur in the dark. "I hate confined spaces because of Sebastian."

Tomas' fingers trailed along her spine. He spoke in her ear. "Why?"

She heaved a deep sigh, hesitant to unburden but needing to. "Whenever he wanted to assert his dominance over me, he would lock me in our bathroom. Sometimes…it was for a few minutes and other times for much longer than that. Now, whenever I'm in a bathroom, I always leave the door open."

Tomas shifted their bodies so he could look at her face in the moonlight. "Oh, God. Baby, I'm so sorry for everything he put you through. Not all men are like that. I'm not like that. Tell me what it's like for you."

She stroked his face with her fingertips. "My heart pounds, I break out in sweats, and it's so hard to draw in a breath. The fear is overwhelming and the only thing I can focus on is being free of the four walls closing in on me." She paused. "You're good, Tomas, through and through. From your soft heart to your pure soul, you're a sensitive and kind gentleman. I appreciate you."

"I'm happy you turned to me during this whole mess, Nahla." His soft lips grazed her forehead. "More grateful and happy than you may ever know."

He held her tightly in his arms, not saying a word as she drifted off to sleep. When she awoke hours later, she was alone in her bed. The pillows still held his scent and she buried her face in each one of them as the tears flooded her eyes and rained down her cheeks. This was the goodbye she had feared.

Nahla ended the call with her relieved mother. She was expected home within a few days. Checking her flight information for a few days later on her cell phone took a moment. She would be leaving the mystic Autumn Moon Inn and Catnip, heading back to the life she had once felt so much joy in.

She took a leisurely shower and put on a cinnamon brown warm and comfy wool dress, pairing them with black boots. It amazed her that she hadn't taken any pleasure in dressing up and applying makeup since her nightmare situation with Sebastian had begun. She felt pretty and relaxed. *And lonely without Tomas...* She brushed away the thought. She had plans to invite him, Lisbeth and Mina to a final breakfast meal before she left. There would be a proper goodbye, she decided.

Locking her room, she headed downstairs to the Cat's Paw Cafe and seated herself. She ordered an herbal tea and perused the menu. The waiter returned and took her order, smiling and praising her food choices. As she sipped her tea, she glanced up at the entrance. Tomas stood there, wearing a lazy smile.

It was a reflex to smile back and he slowly made his way over to the table. She noted how damn hot he looked in his brown sweater and jeans. There was that clean, spicy, masculine scent filling her nose again. He took a seat.

"We're matching colors this morning," she mused.

Those expressive eyes looked hungry and not for food. He subtly winked. "Maybe we're in tune with each other."

She lowered her eyes to the table. 'Could be now that you have your magick back."

He cleared his throat and she could feel his gaze on her. She looked up. "Having my magick is...amazing. But, it's not everything. I still have the loneliness to deal with. I haven't felt that way since you've been here."

"Maybe you need to stop working so much and meet some new people." Her reply was tart.

He chuckled. "Hm. My runaway witch has some sass. No, I was thinking more like I need to continue to cultivate the relationship I have with you."

Nahla's mouth formed a perfect little 'O". She was truly speechless.

"Do you love me?" His soulful eyes searched her face. 'Whether or not you say yes, you should know that I love you, Nahla."

Tears sprang to her eyes. She covered her mouth, nodding. "I do. May the spirits help us both, but I do."

He caught her hand and kissed it, closing his eyes for a moment. "Then, don't run away to Los Angeles." He reached in his pocket and placed a neat black box on the table. He inched it across to her.

She looked at him in amazement and opened the box, revealing a gold ring with a square diamond and a small pearl on each side. "Is this...a gift?"

"It's more than that. This is my grandmother's engagement ring. I'm giving it to you as a promise to love, honor, and cherish you as my wife, if you'll accept it. I want more than a fling. I...want forever with you." He moved from his chair to balance on one knee in front of her.

Nahla wiped the tears from her eyes. "Oh, God, yes! I want my forever to be with you, too. I love you, Tomas Castillo." She noticed the stares from the customers around them and, as he slipped the ring on her finger, there was light applause and a few whistles of good fortune.

"Can you handle more than just me? My baby and I are a package deal."

"He's already mine, too. We'll raise him together here in Catnip, if you want."

"I love it here. Yes, let's stay here and raise our family."

Those expressive eyes held a hint of mischief. "I've pretty much mastered that candle lighting trick, by the way. Let me show you."

Glancing over at the doorway, she noticed Drew Winchester giving them a thumbs up with a beaming smile. She waved back, flashing her ring. Tomas rose to his feet and she put a finger to his lips. "Honey, when we're in private, you can light all my candles. And, you'll be the only one to."

NINE

Autumn Moon Inn, Catnip – One Year Later

"Oh, look at my ninja," Nahla's mother exclaimed, adjusting her pearl encrusted tiara. "You're getting married for real, this time."

Nahla smiled serenely, looking at their reflections in the full- length mirror. They were preparing for her walk down the aisle in her room at the Autumn Moon Inn. The nuptials would take place on the expansive back lawn at the inn. Gilda wore a chic blue suit and she appeared to be happiest she had seen her in a long time.

Nahla gave her reflection a slow inspection, starting from the delicate satin heels, decorated with pearls. She drank in the long white satin and lace dress, with a cinched tight corset and spaghetti straps. Her hair was piled up in a mass of curls with the tiara as an added touch of sleek elegance. When she was satisfied, she turned to face her mother, tearing up a little.

"Stop, Mom. You're making me cry."

"Well, it's true. Sebastian rushing you away for some cheap and illegal ceremony in Las Vegas was enough to make me cry." She glanced at her watch. "It's just about time for your grand entrance."

Nahla moved to the window. She and Tomas had both opted for a small, intimate ceremony at dusk, but all the chairs were full of people in his life who wanted to be a part of the celebration. Looking off into the distance, she watched as Lisbeth, also dressed in blue, placed her infant son in the small wagon for his big moment. She laughed and pointed it out to her mom. Her heart stopped at the sight of Tomas in his navy blue suit, hair neatly combed, waiting for her at the steps of the gazebo.

Baby Kit had made his arrival several months ago right on time, with Tomas clutching her hand through every push and groan. Never had she imagined how much he had invested in his new family. His love and protection were evident every time he kissed her passionately or lifted their son in his arms.

Her mother patted her hand as the violinists began the wedding march song. "It's time, baby."

The moment the pastor from the Witches Council pronounced them husband and wife, Tomas swept her in his embrace and kissed her in a way that was far from chaste. Yells and cheers went up from the guests and Nahla blushed as they came up for air.

"I've been dying to do that since the moment you started down the aisle in that dress," Tomas whispered in her ear. "My wife. My world. My joy."

Nahla leaned into him and addressed the guests. "Thank you all for bearing with us when it comes to the exchange of rings. Our son, the ring boy, had some technical issues."

They looked down the aisle of grass as Mina, in a blue lace dress, pulled the wagon with one hand and tossed flowers with the other. For the first time that day, Kit had stopped crying and wore a huge grin. He shook the blue ribbon with the rings attached in his tiny fist.

Tomas stepped down from the gazebo decorated with fresh flowers and took the rings from Kit, kissing the baby's forehead. He rejoined his bride and slipped the simple white gold band on her finger. She took the matching band and placed it on his finger. More cheers went up from the guests as he kissed her again.

"I can't believe I'm your wife," Nahla whispered in his ear.

After the ceremony, Tomas and Nahla made the rounds, greeting the guests. She had no idea that her new husband was so well loved by such an eclectic group of people. Vampires, as well as many witches from different covens, had shown up to wish them well on their special day.

They were thanking a couple when Nahla caught a tall, well-built man in her peripheral vision, intuiting him to be a vamp. She turned to see Tomas quickly pull him into an embrace.

"Didn't think you were going to make it, old friend."

The vamp, with short black hair and piercing blue eyes, stepped back and grinned. "I didn't miss the vows, man." He turned his smile to Nahla. "Now, you're stuck with him. You'll always be on his sofa as he picks apart your emotional flaws. Life with a therapist."

Nahla giggled, utterly charmed by this stranger. "I'm Nahla Castillo."

The vamp kissed her hand lightly. "I'm Jason Cross, one of Tomas' oldest and dearest friends."

Tomas chuckled. "The pain in my ass, more like." His expression sobered. "You're aware of what's happened here?"

Jason's look was grim. "More than aware. The Vampire Council has had me on the case of this lethal vampire faction for a few months. I'm headed back to L.A. to meet with them about my findings. Caldecott's involvement, a warlock, is going to cause some unrest." He turned his gaze to Nahla. "I only know a little about what you told the authorities, but it sounds like big trouble."

Nahla clutched Tomas' hand as she explained her frightening vision to Jason. He nodded, rubbing his bristled chin thoughtfully. "The long, silver blonde hair is a red flag. I've only known one person who fits your description. It's the vampire queen, ex-queen. Galina Saburova. She was sentenced to blood draining and burial in a secret location over a year ago. It would've killed a lesser vampire."

Nahla tensed, sensing trouble on the horizon. "The spirits are in an uproar about her. The warnings from them now make sense. She is concentrated evil. And, I sense she is far from dead."

Jason swore under his breath. "I'll share what you've told me with the Vampire Council once I'm back in L.A. I also have a witch contact there who can help."

Tomas' lips curved upward. "And, would that be the gracious Pandora?"

Jason snorted. "You mean the Pandora who hates me with the fury of a thousand suns? Yeah. Her."

Tomas kissed her cheek. "I'll fill you in on all this later."

Jason smiled. "Don't take my problems with you on your honeymoon. You two are officially out of this situation. This is my game, now."

Nahla heaved a sigh of relief. She and Tomas didn't have to deal with the nightmare anymore and had a beautiful future waiting.

———

Kauai, Hawaii

Baby Kit squealed with delight as the foamy waves doused his tiny feet and he bounced up and down. Nahla and Tomas stood on either side of him, holding his arms. Birthing him at the hospital in Burlington had taken several painful hours, but all that was forgotten when she and Tomas had gazed in wonder at his perfect face for the first time. In looks, he had taken most of Nahla's features and dark coloring, for which she was thankful. She wanted zero reminders of Sebastian.

Nahla spied her Underground friend, Joseph, making his way down the beach toward them. They pulled Kit away from the water as he approached.

"My fiancée and I are thrilled you made it back here to our sunny shores and not alone this time." He nodded his head at Tomas, who grinned in response. The two men shook hands.

Nahla's laugh was gleeful. "No, I'll never be alone again. I'm overjoyed to be sharing the waves and gorgeous sunsets with my new husband and son."

Joseph stepped forward and draped their necks with colorful, fragrant leis. "Welcome back. We hope to see you as often as possible." He gestured at the Wicked Chicken in the distance. "You'll get a chance to meet my fiancée tonight, if you'd like to join us for dinner."

"We'd love to join you. I'm so excited to meet the woman who stole the heart of the most eligible bartender on the island."

After a few moments of conversation, Joseph bid them goodbye with a wave and lumbered back up the beach.

"This is the perfect honeymoon I always dreamed about." She sighed in contentment.

Kit fussed at her feet and she lifted him in her arms. He put his face in the crook of her neck, sucking his little thumb.

Tomas leaned over and kissed them both. "I'm happy I could give you all this, Nahla."

"Next vacation we need to make time to visit Lisbeth and Mina in their new home in Colorado. I really miss them."

Tomas slipped her hand in his as they strolled leisurely down the beach. "I miss them, too. Tell me, do you miss living in L.A.?"

"I miss living close to mom, but she's only a phone call and plane ride away. I don't miss one single thing about L.A. since I relocated. I love waking up with you in our little home in Catnip. I love you, Tomas."

He stopped walking and caught her lips in a deep kiss. "I can't believe I finally caught my little runaway witch."

Nahla gasped as his tongue teased the shell of her ear. "I chased you until you caught me. And, that's the best thing I ever did."

After another hour of the beach and the crashing waves, they made their way back up to the resort's back entrance. Tomas held little Kit as they walked through the lobby toward the elevators. He pushed the up button and reached out a free hand to Nahla. She gripped it tightly, her gaze focused on the floor.

The doors slid open and he gently tugged her inside.

"Come on, baby. You can do this again. We did it earlier today, remember?"

Nahla nodded as the doors closed and she wrapped her arms around him, burying her face in his neck. Her pulse pounded but, thank God, she was managing it now. Kit's excited babbling was a welcome distraction. As the car ascended to the upper floors, Tomas kissed her forehead.

The elevator came to a stop on their floor and the doors parted. She exited in a rush, looking back to see him right behind her. He slid an arm around her shoulders to calm her slight trembling. "You made it and you're okay. And, we'll keep doing it together until you conquer the fear."

Nahla's eyes welled up with happy tears as they walked down the hallway to their room. "I'm glad I sought professional help. As my counselor, you know exactly what I need."

Tomas' broad grin made her heart catch. "In my professional opinion, everything we both need is right here."

THE END

———

Coming in 2021!
Dark Magic & Dirty Secrets, Spellbound Underground-Bk2

———

Turn the page to read
the first chapter of *Crimson* by Tamela Miles

———

Don't miss out on your next favorite book!

Join the Satin Romance mailing list
www.satinromance.com/mail.html

THANK YOU FOR READING

Did you enjoy this book?

We invite you to leave a review at your favorite book site, such as Goodreads, Amazon, Barnes & Noble, etc.

DID YOU KNOW THAT LEAVING A REVIEW...

- Helps other readers find books they may enjoy.
- Gives you a chance to let your voice be heard.
- Gives authors recognition for their hard work.
- Doesn't have to be long. A sentence or two about why you liked the book will do.

CRIMSON BY TAMELA MILES
CHAPTER ONE

"Oh, hurry the hell up," Delilah muttered under her breath, kneading the small black knit bag with nervous hands. She glanced around the place, taking in the dim lighting and scuffed hardwood floors of a bar named Vivian's in a not-so-great area of Downtown Los Angeles. The dark alley she had passed on the way in reeked of hard liquor and rotten food. She had noted, with pity, the few homeless souls taking refuge next to a large dumpster.

She had been waiting here for what seemed like hours for an acquaintance of her younger brother. She was here to handle another one of Declan's situations because he couldn't handle money responsibly. No, she corrected herself. She was here because she felt slightly guilty saying no to Declan whenever he made too many bad bets, which was often. She recognized that he had a gambling problem. It was definitely time to stop babying him before they both ended up like the homeless people outside. Maybe she should even seek professional counseling for him. Her help didn't seem to be enough.

Her eyes darted around the place, pointedly avoiding the lecherous smiles she was getting from a few of the male patrons. No way in hell did she want to be here too late into the evening, she thought, as the bar's main door opened, letting in a rowdy bunch of people. She could see it was well beyond dusk through the door.

Her gaze settled on one of the men who stepped away from the crowd and looked around the place slowly. He was tall and powerfully built in jeans and leather jacket with the interior lights glinted off his close cropped blond hair. He had already captured most of the female attention in the bar as their heads turned. Not wanting to be caught staring, she glanced away. *The mysterious Ash Lockler, maybe?*

———

Ash had entered the bar in an unobtrusive effort, right behind the raucous crowd of people. His way was to enter a scene quietly, keeping to the shadows of a room. He had to make this quick. This was a simple business transaction and as long as the woman also saw it as such, the smoother things would be.

He saw her right away, the sister. The resemblance between Declan McDade and his sister, the lovely Delilah, was marked. They shared the same dark, curly hair and olive skin. She twisted the long brown strands around two fingers and looked around anxiously.

His smile was small and grim. Declan had become an annoyance and Ash had little patience with him. He wouldn't keep her waiting and approached her table slowly.

"Ash Lockler?" she said, looking up at him. She looked

away from his intense gaze for a moment. Clearing her throat, she met his eyes again.

Ash nodded and neatly folded his big frame into the booth, opposite her. He maintained his poker face as he rested his forearms on the table, hands folded. He held her gaze for a moment before he spoke quietly. "I trust you will provide what I expect." He surveyed her pretty face framed by all that long, wildly curly, dark hair. She would do nicely.

Her lips parted to speak, but she hesitated for a moment before nodding slowly. He found her actions amusing, assuming this was her first time in dealing with someone like him. The underworld of vampires and other nocturnal beings was definitely not for this little, gentle mouse. She was beautiful but too timid and nervous for his taste. He caught her staring before she lowered her gaze and reached for her small knit bag.

"Yes. I have it right here. Five thousand cash. You can count it. That should settle my brother's debt to you."

Ash's eyes narrowed in irritation. Declan McDade. The little weasel. Unfortunately for his family, he had grown up to be exactly like his father, Martin. They both shared an unhealthy fascination with underworld dealings. His next words were measured. "I'm afraid that five thousand doesn't even come close to what your brother owes me. His debt is a lot closer to one hundred thousand."

Her lips went slack, and she promptly snapped her mouth shut.

Ash went on. "Your money, in short, is no good. A different sort of payment was arranged between myself and Declan."

"What do you want, then? My house?" Delilah's voice was strangely hoarse, and she took a hasty sip of water.

"No, your house is safe. I want your body on a long- term basis. Anywhere from six months to one year would work," Ash replied simply. She was a blood donor to settle a debt and nothing more, he reminded himself.

The water flew out of her mouth before she could stop it. She wiped her mouth with her fingers. "I'm sorry. Did you just say you want my body?"

Ash nodded, his focus on her full, ripe lips for a few seconds, while he watched a myriad of emotions play across her face. He sensed her shock and anger as her eyes narrowed.

She murmured softly, as if to herself. "This is it − the horrible moment I've always feared. Declan's gambling and whoring has come back to bite us in the ass." Aloud, her tone frosty and expression stony, she told him, "It's not that kind of party, Mr. Lockler." She grabbed her little black bag and left the booth, heading for the main door of the bar.

Ash sighed, rubbing the bridge of his nose in aggravation. Declan McDade had caused him too much inconvenience for quite some time, which was not only sad but dangerous. The kid should be focused on making something good of himself, not living on exorbitant amounts of borrowed cash to fund his debauchery. Maybe it was time for him to just be dead and Ash wouldn't have to deal with this shit anymore. You didn't live as long as he had without knowing a little something about how human emotions work. Surprisingly, the remaining water in her glass hadn't splashed in his face.

He watched Delilah's hips sway in her grey sweater dress and black heels as she exited the bar and he moved quickly to catch her. A woman walking alone at night in this rundown area was begging for trouble.

Delilah was halfway across the crowded parking lot before he gripped her arm. She whipped around, and he instantly felt like one of those pushy people who couldn't let things go and take a simple no for an answer. "Let me go!"

"Declan will pay that debt, one way or the other," Ash said coldly. "I think you would both rather not find out how severe the consequences can be if not."

"Are you threatening us? I offered you five thousand dollars, but my body is not for settling debts. Take what I have and leave us alone."

Ash didn't relish the thought of glamouring her, but he was starving. Untainted human blood was very hard to come by and it was superior in every way to animal blood. He caught her arms and pulled her roughly to him. He smiled and caught her big brown eyes with his. "I'm not going to hurt you and you have no reason to fear me. You and Declan have both known me for years, though you rarely see me." He paused, gauging her facial expressions to see if she was under the spell of his calm, softly spoken words. Now that he had seen her snippy side, some perverse side of him wanted to see how far he could take this with his lies. He was mildly fascinated by her for the moment.

"There's always been an unspoken attraction between you and me, Delilah. We've never explored it, which is probably wise, considering that, if you would let me, I would have you in your home, in the backseat of your car, or up against the wall in the alley. We can argue here in a cold parking lot or we can talk this through at your place. Your choice." He had no intention of trying to screw her, of course. He had plenty of willing female vampires for that. This was all about the blood lust.

He could see she was drowning in his focused gaze. Her

knees wobbled, and he held her up. He knew her whole being was focused on his eyes and the cadence of his words. She nodded in acquiescence. "We can go to my home." She paused, looking dazed as she licked her lips. He followed the unconsciously seductive movement with his eyes. "Ash, I feel like…I haven't seen you in a long time," she said.

Ash gave her a reassuring smile. "Yes, Delilah, it's been a long time since we've seen each other. It's the nature of the business I handle, and I wouldn't be here now if it wasn't for Declan's trouble. We'll talk later at your place. You look a little sick. Give me your keys and I'll drive."

———

They were in her house, a modest beige townhouse in Pasadena not far from the Rose Bowl. On arriving, she had invited him in without giving it a second thought. Of course, she was still under the mistaken belief they were old friends. On the drive over, he had concocted an entire history of their friendship, including a friendship with her brother.

"So many vampire books," Ash murmured as he scanned Delilah's crammed bookshelves. There was a small collection of romance novels and thrillers, but there were far more books about vampires.

Delilah smiled and moved to stand next to Ash as she sipped from her glass of red wine. "Vampires are a passion of mine. I thought you knew that about me." Her tone was questioning.

"I was just remarking that there seem to be even more vampire books than the last time I was here," Ash replied smoothly. He picked a book from one of the shelves and read the title aloud. "Blood Lust of the Damned." He snorted. "How appropriate."

His thirst for her blood wasn't easily controlled but he was managing it for the moment. The sweet smell of it pulsing through her veins reminded him why he was willing to settle the exorbitant debt in exchange for her donations. His gaze settled on Delilah's face and he found himself deeply curious about her.

From the dreamy look on her face, he knew she was swimming in a fathomless depth like every human who had been glamoured. He still recalled the dazed feeling of the hypnotic pull before he had been turned. It made one's thoughts disjointed and prevented focusing on one particular notion for very long. It also lowered inhibitions. As he continued to examine her books, his mind conjured up images of his pale skin next to her darker skin as he kissed her. He pushed down his urges.

"Would you like a glass of wine?" She moved away from him and he suspected she was trying to get out of his disturbing orbit, so she could think clearly. He knew her concentration was shot.

"No, thank you," Ash responded, his tone distracted. He shifted his gaze from the books to watch her closely as she sat down on the sofa.

"Have a seat, Ash. Your flight to Denver doesn't leave for a few hours." He sat on a red chair directly across from her and Delilah smiled warmly. "Are you pale all over?"

His eyes were drawn to the contrast of her dark hair and dress against the deep rich red of her sofa. Delilah McDade was an enchanting little thing and snippy as hell when she wasn't glamoured. Her home was also a pleasant surprise, done in crimson and black rather than boring shades of brown and taupe. The colors spoke to him since his own expensive loft in Downtown Los Angeles was decorated completely in black.

"I don't like the sun much."

"Are those beautiful green eyes really contact lenses?"

"All me."

"Why are you so cold? I mean, your skin is practically sub-zero."

"Low blood pressure."

"Will you kiss me?"

Ash hesitated before answering. "As much as I'd really like to, I'm going to say no. Your brother wouldn't appreciate one of his oldest friends hitting on his sister."

Delilah moved without a word and stood directly in front of him. "I'm going to sit in your lap, Ash, and you're going to tell me exactly why we shouldn't be more than friends." She straddled his legs and wrapped her arms around his shoulders. "I've known you forever. Isn't this the next logical step?"

Ash's eyes narrowed thoughtfully. This was a perfect position to simply take what he needed. Very soon, he would be caught up in bloodlust as he'd nearly been back in the parking lot earlier. He smiled at Delilah disarmingly, first stroking her dark hair and then trailing his fingers down her neck. He genuinely liked her. Remarkably, even though he had only known for a couple of hours, she was becoming more than just a blood bag to him. He would take what he needed for the moment and not a drop more. He kissed her neck, and she moaned softly in his ear.

She seemed to thoroughly enjoy his soft, cool lips leaving a trail of goosebumps along her neck. She shivered against him as his tongue traced the shell of her ear. He was about to devour her gorgeous lips when she suddenly pulled away from him. She slapped him. Hard. His fangs shot out immediately and he growled menacingly low in this throat. He grabbed her shoulders.

Delilah gasped in wonder, reaching up to stroke one of his fangs gently. "Vampire," she said in breathless delight. "I was dead on right about you. You are real. My Grammy was from New Orleans, and she told me and my brother all the myths of Southern vampire kingdoms."

Ash shook his head. "The Southern vampire kingdoms are far from a myth. They have existed in secret for centuries and even though every state in the U.S. is now under the rule of one powerful vampire, it wasn't always that way. Your grandmother probably had underground connections to know what she did."

Delilah smiled in remembrance. "Knowing Grammy, I'm certain she did. She insisted she had even met a few in her youth that had her all hot and bothered but we thought she was just telling us a good story." She shook her head slowly. "I'm still not sure if vamps are part of religious folklore or victims of a rare blood disease."

Ash swore under his breath. "A lot of both, but I've never had a crucifix burn me, though I doubt if any of us are God's favorite creatures. Did your grandmother also warn you about the true nature of every vampire? Blood lust rules us at times and it's serious business." His voice was chiding. "Delilah, this is nothing new. You've always known we're real."

She frowned in confusion. He knew she was trying to sort it all out. He was a true life vampire and everything she had dreamed about them was now a part of her reality. "I guess I've always known deep down. My mind is a little cottony right now on some of the details of our friendship, but does Declan know?"

"Yes, of course he knows. Your brother has been involved in some underworld dealings for quite some time. I don't want you to have the mistaken impression that I took advantage by bringing his debt into a situation without him having full disclosure."

She sighed. "No, Declan can easily find trouble on his own. Are there many more of you? Tell me everything." Delilah wrapped her arms around him tightly, resting her face in the crook of his neck and the radiating warmth of her thighs stiffened his cock. He was fighting a losing battle, even though she was only supposed to feed him. Getting sexual with her was definitely a bad idea.

He kept his voice gentle. "You already know everything about me. You just have to remember."

"Well, you'll have to tell me again," she demanded playfully.

Ash's voice was soft and thoughtful as he told her stories of his past. She hung on every word and he caught glimpses of the child she had been. He knew she was in her early thirties with Declan about ten years behind her. He could easily picture what she would look like as an old woman. And, where would he be? Somewhere still under the thumb of the Vampire Council and still trying to come to grips with what he was.

"Tell me more about your past before you became a bad-ass vamp," Delilah said eagerly, still straddling him.

Ash's lip tilted up slightly at the pet name she had adopted for his kind. "I was born Asher John Lockler in 1918. The small town I lived in—Caddo, far up in Northern California —has prospered and is still around today, but I won't dare go back to try to find any of my living family in the foreseeable future. I can't risk being recognized. I am an only child, a miracle child born late in life to my parents, who are buried there. I was turned by my maker when I was 20." He sighed. "Enough talk." He pulled her close and nuzzled her neck.

"Oh, if you need to feed…" Delilah tilted her head back, exposing her throat.

"You would willingly let me feed from you?"

"Of course. What's a little blood between friends?" she quipped.

He laughed at that. Curiosity struck him again, and he pulled back a little. "What do you do for a living now, Delilah?" He watched the fleeting trace of disappointment on her face and laughed inwardly. So eager to be so close to death. He didn't lie to himself. He knew what he was. A little more information about her was all he wanted. His thirst was nearly raging, but he found he needed to satisfy his intense desire to know more about her before taking her blood.

"I'm still a toy design consultant for Kinder Fun," Delilah said. At his blank look, she explained more in detail. "Know that child's game, Bouncin' Blocks? All my work. I created that." She sounded proud of her accomplishment.

Ash nodded in understanding. "Sounds like you're doing well for yourself." He looked around her place again, cataloging every book, rug, and throw pillow.

"After six years at the university earning both of my degrees, I expect nothing less," she replied. She placed her head on his shoulder.

He stroked her hair and she sighed in contentment.

"I take it that a husband and the birth of children will be next for you?" he asked softly, trailing his fingers down her spine. She shivered a bit at his touch.

"Soon, but not now. There's quite a lot I want to do with my life. Then there's Declan to take care of."

The thought of Declan taking advantage of her, even in small ways, pissed him off a little. He had quickly offered up his sister as a blood donor and sex partner to settle a huge debt and had probably expected Delilah to comply. He was nothing more than a low lying snake in high grass, as far as Ash was concerned. He would glamour him later. "Parenthood is a joy that I will probably never experience. I envy you."

"Vamps can't make babies?" Delilah asked slowly.

He shrugged. "I've never tried but it has happened. I suppose if my body temperature was ever warm enough my seed could produce a child. Highly improbable, though."

He kissed the palm of her hand, eyes closed. She planted little kisses on his neck. Ash withstood the sweet torment before his control broke and he kissed her roughly. The moment his tongue met hers, he was overwhelmed by the need to touch her everywhere, to take her. He knew her thoughts were still in a jumble, but he was sure she wanted him just as badly.

Ash quickly unbuttoned the top of her sweater dress, impatiently pushing it down around her waist. Her bra was black lace and he took a moment to appreciate it before unclasping the front, baring her breasts. Shame he would never see the panties. "This will hurt," he said softly as he sank his fangs into the side of one lovely breast. She gasped in shock.

Ash sank into the sweetest maelstrom ever. Her blood was like fragrant honey and drawing blood from her had his skin burning all over, while his cock stiffened against her. She ground her hips and he knew the slight sting of his fangs buried in her skin created a tingling in her core by the faint scent of her arousal. She cupped his head in her hands and murmured encouraging words. He continued until she told him she was dizzy. He retracted his fangs and pulled back to look at her, his lips stained with her blood.

"That was unforgettable. I think that was an orgasm," Delilah said, licking her parched lips. She struggled to stay awake, but her eyelids kept closing. She rested her head on his shoulder as he closed her bra and dress, placing her on the sofa. He watched her drifting off and leaned down to speak softly in her ear.

"Don't worry about your brother's debt. I'll handle everything as an old friend. Consider it paid in full."

He leaned over and kissed her forehead. He didn't dare linger. His thirst had been quenched and she had aroused another great need. He would quickly find another willing human blood donor and sex partner, though finding one to suit his long-term arrangement would be a bit more difficult. Delilah deserved far better than the arrangement he had proposed. She worked hard to support herself and her brother and there was no way in hell she could afford to give him nearly one hundred thousand dollars. He now considered the debt paid in full.

He thought about glamouring her again, to completely erase all of her memories of him and this night. He decided to leave things as they were. He wanted her to remember the one, hot night with a vampire he had given her until she was old woman, telling old stories about his kind, like her Southern grandmother.

Ash left her sleeping and opened her front door. Back to his real life as an undead, such as it was. He was still very much owned by the Vampire Council and his queen. One didn't ignore a summons from them, leaving no place in his life for tender things.

ABOUT THE AUTHOR

Tamela Miles Tamela Miles is a school psychologist with Ed.S and PPS credential and a graduate of California State University San Bernardino and California State University Dominguez Hills. She is also a former flight attendant. She grew up in Altadena, California in that tumultuous time known as the 1980s. She now resides with her family in the Inland Empire, CA. She's a horror/paranormal romance writer mainly because it feels so good having her characters do bad things and, later, pondering what makes them so bad and why they can never seem to change their wicked ways.

She enjoys emails from people who like her work.
In fact, she loves emails.
She can be contacted at tamelamiles@yahoo.com
or her Facebook page, Tamela Miles Books.

She also welcomes reader reviews and enjoys the feedback from people who love to read as much as she does.

https://allauthor.com/author/tamelamiles

facebook.com/sassysleepingbeauties

twitter.com/jackiebrown20

instagram.com/tamelamilesbooks

bookbub.com/authors/tamela-miles

ALSO BY TAMELA MILES

Crimson